REHAB

KENNA KAY

Rehab

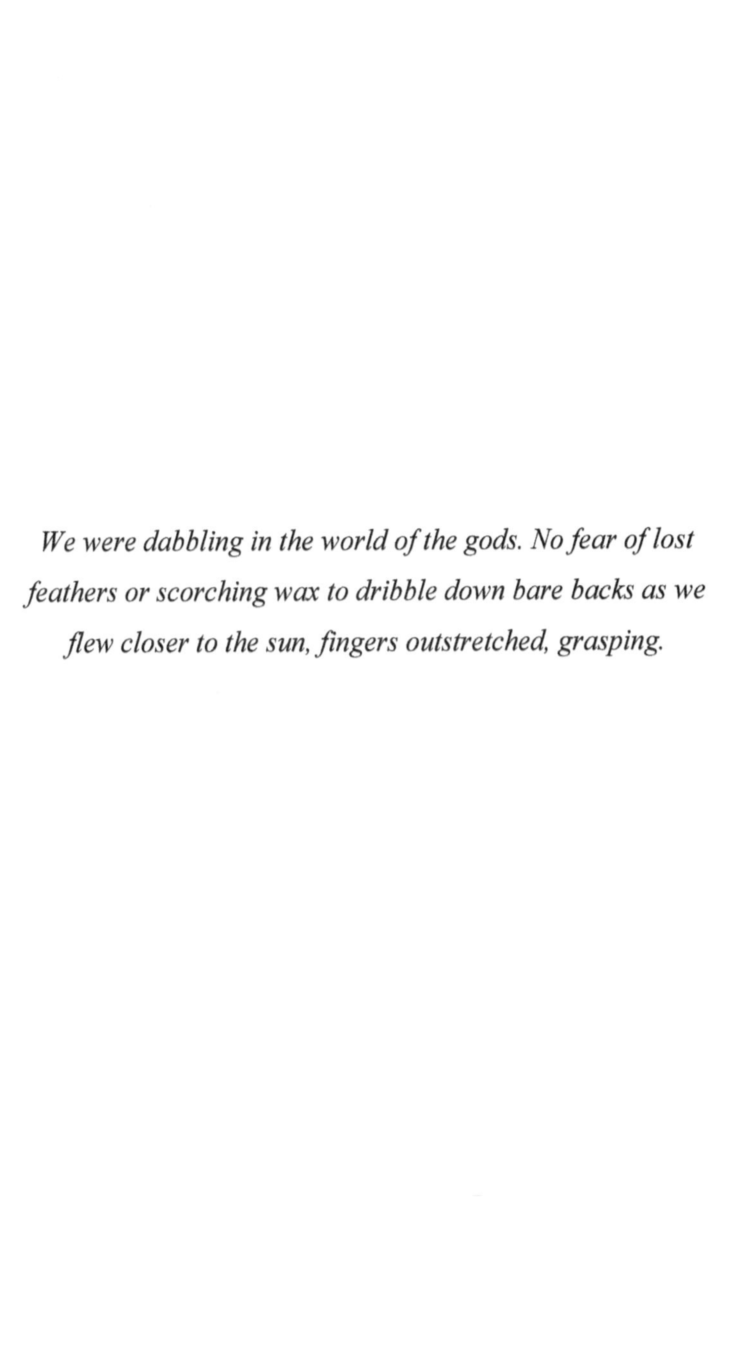

We were dabbling in the world of the gods. No fear of lost feathers or scorching wax to dribble down bare backs as we flew closer to the sun, fingers outstretched, grasping.

Juliet

When love leaves, it takes much more with it than it gave. The bedsheets are cold. My fingers twitch next to me, aching to reach out for the warmth that isn't there. He was there a minute ago, his face searching mine.

Mom is standing in the doorway, the crack casting a sliver of light into my room that cuts through the dark. In it, each dust particle is frozen in ambience. Her voice is a murmur, an ocean away. There's another voice in the hallway, and movement on the other side of the bed. I can tell it is Sophie because it is too light to be him.

"Jules, I think it's time to get up." Sophie's voice is gentle in the dark. Its familiarity cuts through my haze of sleep. She lies where he once did. Her eyes skip between my own, trying to untangle me.

Sophie's eyes have always changed color, even when we were children, forever framed by her honey curls. Green like the garden's lily pads one day, and gold like the harvest the next.

"Let's go get help," she prompts, this time holding back tears.

I know. My eyes close in a half wince. *But I can't.* There is no strength, not even from deep within me, to stand, pull the curtains aside, and leave this room. Guilt pits itself inside my stomach.

I have let them all down.

"Just get up, Jules," Sophie tries again. My oldest friend… Mom was smart to ask her for help.

I will get up. I will get up. I will get up. When I open my eyes, he is where she was.

He smiles with the corners of his mouth; it is small and kind, for me. *"Come on, Jules, get up,"* he says.

A warm hand slips into mine and pulls. I get up.

"I promise this will make you feel better," Sophie chides while glancing back at me, careful not to walk too fast or too far ahead on the concrete path, like she is worried she'll blink and I'll be gone. The walking has tired my legs after days of not moving. My eyes hurt in the brightness of daylight. The dullness in my chest has changed into a crushing sensation, as if something heavy is sitting on me, testing my ribs and pushing down on my lungs. And the ache, it is constant. I could easily swallow a pill for it, but choose not to. I think of what I would say if I had the breath.

I am too tired to fight, Soph.

When the Clinic finally comes into view, its size stops me mid-stride. It looms in front of us, a concrete shape of tinted windows and brutalist architecture, big enough to block out the afternoon sun, casting shadows down onto itself. From where we stand at the bottom of the steps, there is no sky. Sophie grabs my hand, pulling me forward towards its waiting doors. They open for us when we are close enough.

Inside, we are greeted by a rush of cool air. A sharp contrast to its exterior, the interior of the Clinic is warm and welcoming. Spotless and pristine, the lobby is all windows and beams of dark wood that stretch from the floor to the vaulted ceilings, washing the room in sunlight. Waiting patients fill the chairs lining the sides of the room, their chatter a light buzz that fills the space. They are all smiles and straight backs.

Am I the only sick one?

Sophie is nearly to the front desk, no longer at my side. I catch up and slide next to her. Behind the desk, a set of double doors stare at me; their frosted glass gives nothing away. The receptionist finishes her call and puts a finger to her earpiece. She looks up with a smile. She's young, but not too young. Her chestnut hair is pulled back in a glossy ponytail, eyes bright behind her glasses.

"Hi, Tracy." Sophie grins, setting her elbows on the desk.

"Hi, Sophie, back for Therapy?" Tracy asks, still smiling, acting as if they are old friends. "There's a group session starting right now. You're just in time to catch it."

"No Therapy today," Sophie says apologetically. "I brought someone new to treatment." Sophie moves aside so Tracy can see me. "This is my friend, Juliet."

Her eyes bore into mine as she flashes the same smile. *"Perfect!"* It is too broad to be genuine. "I'll get you registered here, then assign you a nurse technician in the back. They'll determine your level of care then. Scan here," Tracy instructs, tapping the glass embedded in the desktop. I swipe my wrist over the scanner, my raised lines of embedded nanotech just brushing the surface. After a moment, the screen glows green, and the desk holo projects my community profile into the air. With a few taps of her finger, Tracy registers my file. She gives it a final swipe, sending the holo back into the desk. "All done." She beams, then stands. "I'll walk you back."

With each heartbeat, my chest grows tight and pained.

I got this far with Sophie pulling me along.

I can still leave. I pause, looking at the double doors that will lead me into the Clinic. Is it better to walk away and feel everything, or to stay and feel nothing at all? I have always set a firm boundary between myself and the innovation presented by our Community. I was one of the few who silently refused the Clinic, but desperation brought me here. *In a world of technology, where do we draw our line?*

Before I can decide, Sophie grasps my hand. She's nodding at me with a hopeful smile that touches her eyes. "Just heal, okay?" she says.

I nod without heart. With a final squeeze, Sophie lets go. My chest continues to shrink, my heartbeat in my ears.

"Right through here." Tracy holds the door open for me. I move to follow her. The same smile is still pasted on her face, impossibly wide and unbending.

Did the Clinic do that?

Unease pits in my stomach. Behind us, the doors slide shut, clicking into place, silencing the noise and light of the lobby.

Inside, the Clinic is a labyrinth of glass hallways and obscured doors, each step giving way to another section of the building identical to the last. Sunlight pours into the intricate hallways, its rays warm against my skin. Through the glass, I can see the smaller rooms outside that stem from the doors, their walls white and concrete like the main building. Each click of Tracy's heels echoes on the polished floor. I follow loosely at her side, our reflections trailing beside us. After one more hallway, Tracy stops. Before us is one of the smaller rooms, its door tucked away in the wall, waiting.

"You'll be right in here. Take a seat, get comfortable. Your nurse technician will be with you in a moment," says Tracy. "You'll absolutely love it!"

I give her a nod.

Tracy departs, and soon the click of her heels fades until there is nothing but silence and my twisting stomach. I'm still standing, glued a step past the doorway. The room is four plain walls reflecting the gentle glow of the ceiling lights, the floor a mosaic of polished white tiles. In the corner, a desk and rolling chair are tucked away. At the very center of the room sits a large chair; it looks comfortable, like it is made for relaxing in. As Tracy instructed, I take a seat. It is as comfortable as it looks. I sink into it, its underlying structure molded to cradle a body. I notice the armrests are bare, one a panel of gray metal, the other a glass screen. Before I can study any more, there's a knock on the door. I look up to see a boy who appears to be just older than me. He is a tower of broad shoulders and a mop of dark curls. They remind me of Sophie's love, Elijah.

"Hi, I'm Jona. I'll be your nurse technician." He meets me in two strides, sticking out his hand in greeting. Behind him, the door slides out from the frame, clicking into place. Outside, blurs of light fight against the frosted glass. I feel as if some sort of tether has been cut.

"Juliet," I say, slipping my hand into his, much larger than mine. I let go after a moment.

"It's nice to meet you, Juliet." Jona grabs the desk chair and rolls it across the room so he can sit in front of me.

Wasting no time, he jumps right into it, pulling a tablet out of his white coat, positioning it on his lap. "To start, I'm going to ask you a series of questions to determine your level of care. Some questions may be easier to answer than others. Take the time you need." He glances up to check if I am following. I nod.

Satisfied, he turns back to his tablet. With a tap of his finger, light erupts from its screen, a grid of overlapping blue lines. The holo covers us, mapping our faces and the room, then it disappears, recording.

"Are you here for Rehab or Therapy?"

"Rehab."

"Is the cause of your seeking care male or female?"

"Male."

"Was the relationship mutual, conditional, or unrequited?"

"Mutual."

"And how long since you've last been together? Exact time increment, if possible."

"Seven months and six days."

"Please explain your hurt, to the best of your ability."

This answer does not come immediately. Sadness and heartache weigh heavier inside me. Jona's waiting patiently, his face a perfect mask. He does this every day. Nothing I say will surprise him, but my face still flushes with embarrassment. I look away from him down at my shoes. To have neglected science for seven long months—neglecting *a cure*—is shameful.

"I have the old disease," I start. The room expands with the silence that comes after my admission. "It started with aching joints in my breastbone, just after the breakup. I thought it was how I had been sleeping or sitting, that I had found some position that irritated a lining or ligament. Then the shortness of breath started. When the apathy followed, I knew it wasn't my posture, but him. And soon … I just … stopped getting up." I pause for a shaky breath; my lungs feel too small now, like I cannot get enough air. "I isolated, cut myself off, because it was easier to be alone. If I wasn't asleep, I was awake, reliving *us*, wishing for it back, replaying our last conversation on an impossible-to-stop loop, pushing me further into myself." I had been in the kind of love that turned people inside out when it left. I was a walking heartbreak.

"Why didn't you seek treatment sooner?" There's a slight difference in his face, a tone that wasn't there before. But it's not pity; I think it's curiosity. My guilt and shame soften; in turn, the sadness brews. I can feel it now, sitting there, like a wave in the sea trying to pull me under. I shake my head, eyes closed.

"I thought I could heal on my own," I say, abashed.

"Okay." He speaks with a simple understanding. "Thank you for sharing, for coming here to heal." Jona looks me in the eye, attentive and honest. Somehow, it is a comfort. I almost give him a smile. He taps on his tablet, breaking the moment. "Last question, have you decided on detachment or severance from the root of heartbreak?"

Severance would cut the feelings but keep the person. Mostly parents and persons who have lost their partner go this route, to ease the pain but not truly forget their love. Detachment cuts the person away completely, a stranger forever. For ambient loss, the scornful, those who felt too deeply.

"Detachment."

"Okay." Jona notes. "Before finishing the evaluation, I need to take a physical of your heart." The chair begins to recline, and after a moment of reluctance, I move with it. "Just sit back and relax," Jona says, tapping the screen of his tablet. He holds it over my chest, and I close my eyes and focus on pulling breaths from my diaphragm. In and out … in and out … willing the ache to leave.

"Your heart is about seventy-five percent broken," Jona notes, pulling away.

I know.

Jona taps his tablet again, and a holo shoots into the air, washing the walls with its blue glow. I recognize my heart from the moments I'd checked it myself since losing him. Behind the locked bathroom door, I had watched the organ grow smaller and smaller with use of the medi-kit, replacing it before mom came knocking to check on me, hiding my sickness. I'd watched it shrink until I couldn't take it anymore. To see it now, weakened but pulsating, gives some validation to all the grief I could not shake.

Swiping both his hands away from each other, Jona zooms into the holo, passing through the walls of my heart to reveal a deeper level of the scan: the stringy tissue inside the organ. It pulsates rhythmically with each beat, pumping blood and thin tendons, crisscrossing to hold it all together. "These are your heart strings," Jona points out, touching the tip of his finger to the strands. "These muscles are responsible for contracting and relaxing the heart to pump blood. In severe cardiac cases resulting from emotional trauma, they become weak and prone to breakage. When they break, it can lead to organ failure."

Organ failure. His words ring in the hollows of me.

As if he can sense the weight of his words, he adds, "Nothing a little love can't fix."

It's a joke, but I can't bring myself to smile. Jona powers down the tablet, and the light is gone in an instant. I blink and see the outline of my heart, small and weak. Silence hangs between us while Jona makes notes on the eval.

"Can Rehab really take the pain away?" I ask, cautious.

Jona's eyes catch mine, and he smiles. "I'm proud to say that science can officially cure broken hearts." Each word is genuine. His eyes are kind and eager. I trust him. Maybe it's his broad shoulders and easy smile, remnants of a lost comfort. "Rehab will heal the old disease, the organ failure, your head *and* heart. Should you want to undergo treatment, it will begin with an inpatient stay and a scheduled series of treatment sessions. You'll go through as many sessions as you need for it to take. Like the stages of grief, it takes everyone different time increments. Most people take ten to twenty sessions. Your mind will take what it needs to pass through the grief cycle and, ultimately, acceptance. You'll be completely healed within a month or two." "Healed" meaning completely severed or detached, ignorant and blissful. "After Rehab concludes, you'll receive less frequent sessions of reinforcement Therapy to prevent a relapse." Jona pauses, focusing on his tablet, his fingers dancing across the screen, still logging my data into the Clinic system. "We can begin treatment today. After your evaluation, I recommended it—"

I don't need to think. My heart is at risk. I got up. I am here. That is enough.

"I'd like treatment today," I cut Jona off. He looks up.

"Okay." It is a plain response, an acknowledgment. He taps away. "For the record, then, will you please confirm that you, Juliet, accept Rehab treatment?"

"I, Juliet, accept treatment."

"Preliminary eval concluded," Jona says. The grid reappears and is sucked into the tablet just as promptly, signaling the end of the recording. Jona pockets his tablet. "Let's head on back." He stands to leave, then looks to me, his eyes bright. "Welcome to the Clinic, Juliet."

* * *

"Based on the condition of your heart, we'll start treatment immediately." Jona nods as he talks while I trail behind him through the hallways. "You'll stay in the Clinic until you're deemed healed enough for Therapy. A more in depth informational holo will be sent to your room. It will cover care and daily workings here, outlining the rules and regulations of your time inpatient." He glances back at me and asks if I have any questions yet. I shake my head no.

We continue to walk the hallways, passing through a second set of double doors and into a new wing, stepping right into a common room.

I take in the double ceiling and glossy oak beams that run into the polished wooden floor, similar to the lobby. Light couches frame a brick fireplace. Floor-to-ceiling bay windows on the far side demand the room's attention, giving a full view of Center outside, nestled below the hill. There, the buildings spiral for the sky, a proud display of our architecture. At their feet, the city's waterways catch the colors of the now dying day, lush greenery blending into the sky's evenfall hues, reflecting the trans trac that weaves throughout, defying gravity.

"Welcome to the hospitality wing," Jona finally says, as if he were captivated for a moment by Center as well. "This is the main room. Most Rehab patients lounge here. We encourage you to spend most of your time outside of treatment here and find community in one another. Since you're not allowed to leave the Clinic until after you've finished treatment, we have everything you need here. We have two recreation rooms." He nods to the right at two doors. "We have a fitness room and a fully functioning archive. Most use the archive to help treatment take, reliving the new memory. Come, I'll show you to your room."

I follow Jona as he veers off to the left. There is a small hall-way here; obscured doors line its sides. Between the door-frames, a scanner and plaque are embedded into the wall space.

I notice smooth outlines of letters cut into the plaques. He stops at the last door on the right. I finger my name already on its plaque: JULIET. Not a single rough edge.

"It's programmed to open only to your nanotech, for optimal privacy. Meals are served every four hours in the main room, and you're welcome to explore the activity rooms on the other side of the wing. Tracy can get a hold of me, so if you need anything, let her know. I'll come back in an hour for your first treatment."

I thank Jona and watch him disappear through the doors. When I push my wrist to my door, it glides open without a catch.

The room is just large enough to fit the full-sized bed and a comfortable amount of foot space. The walls are the same plain color as the treatment room, the floor the same polished tile. A holo screen runs across the wall parallel to the door. Below it the bed sits, large and inviting, its bedding cozy and plush, pil-lows piled on top of it against the bed frame. There's an open entryway to a small bathroom with a double sink and mirror that runs the length of the small space. Above, a skylight still pulsates heat from the warm day, casting a square of dulled light onto the floor. The cabinet inside is stocked with Community-sanctioned day clothes, plain pants and shirts in our familiar grays and off-whites. With nothing to do but wait, I crawl into the bed, pulling the covers up to my chin. The ceiling is the same plain color as the walls.

The thoughts come now that I'm alone. *Mom*. She'd been crying days before I left. She felt guilty too, that she could not get me out of bed on her own. I wanted to tell her it wasn't her fault. I was just a romantic; I wanted to heal on my own, how we used to before our science changed everything, before our age of neo-gods. Sophie likes to remind me that that age had passed long ago, all its lesser medicines, sciences, and governments with it.

The informational holo sits on the bed where it has been placed by Clinic staff. I pick it up and turn it over in my hands, a clear screen trimmed in metal. One tap, and it will wake, shooting its programming into the air. I'd found mom's years ago, back when the science had first been introduced to the Community. Even though I was young, I still remember the advertisement: *100% synthetic, 100% real results!* There was even talk about adding a new god to the garden, fashioned in the likeness of the scientist who created Rehab and Therapy. Instead, he was named a grand contributor. I weave the holo between my fingers, then decide to watch it. I tap it against the bed frame, and light bursts from it.

A voice begins to narrate: *"We succeed because we must. On behalf of the Clinic staff, congratulations on taking your first step towards healing. What should you expect in your sessions? A treatment plan specific to you, the patient, carefully constructed by your nurse technician. Every session begins with an evaluation. Your nurse technician will check your emotional, mental, and physical state to adjust and document your healing process accordingly. After injection, you will experience a memory. Memory, like the heart, is a fickle thing. Treatment is different for every patient; whichever memory you see is what your mind needs. In addition to the memory, you will also experience strong feelings and emotions. These feelings and emotions will begin to change by your second treatment, with Rehab conditioning the love away. Do not worry; this is where the healing happens. Upon returning, you will be cleared, then released by your nurse technician."*

A body stands tall in the holo, its chest rising and falling. Complex visuals of bodily systems, nerves, and organs appear. *"The brain is an extraordinary organ. Here at the Clinic, we take advantage of its unique potential in our treatment. How exactly does it work? The special prescription of synthetic love mimics the chemicals and hormones of real love, lodging in your brain's receptors for love. Paired with the root of heartbreak, synthetic love works to diminish the body's natural production of real love at sight of the stimulus."* Then it shows love moving through the bodily system, starting at the injection sight, spreading up the arm to the heart, where its pumping circulates it into every vein, lighting the body up in gold. Once it reaches the brain, a smaller visual appears, showing synthetic love lodging into the brain's receptors like boats into ports, leaving real love with nowhere to go. I let the holo run, it's noise and picture comforting in the silence of the room, but I stop listening. I don't need to see any more.

The Clinic techniques are well-known, complex neuroscience paired with basic psychology and biology, heralded as a perfect harmony of human nature and science. Love is an equation they pulled from our own biological processes that create hormones and emotions, used in both Rehab and Therapy.

Rehab is an inpatient stay until it's completed. Then you are allowed to go home again, only returning to the Clinic for lifelong Therapy sessions, reinforcing Rehab's work. Rehab shows you memories of the loved one you want to detach from, conditioning your body to feel less and less each time you see them, using your own memories and synthetic love to replace the real love you have for them, until there is no real love left. No love, no feelings. The memories turn into dreams, easy to forget after waking, and the object of your love will be a stranger again. After, in Therapy, they will fill you with real love, the good love, showing you memories of your family and friends like a distraction from what you just lost, filling the void you just created. The lucky ones are people like Sophie, who has never had to go to Rehab. She hasn't lost someone yet, and only knows the bliss of Therapy, used to stay in love with her partner.

Treatment plans are vital to healing properly and have to be followed exactly. The Clinic is a controlled environment, with not a single variable out of place. The isolation of Rehab's inpatient stay ensures the treatment will take. For these few weeks, my life will be a series of evaluations and treatments, and in turn, my heart will be healed. The poets, even the oldest, center their art on the broken heart. Seeing my broken heart minutes before with Jona, floating in front of us, weakened yet still pulsating, was a new type of fruition all its own. Grief and broken-heartedness are the strongest feelings man can know. Now, forget. This is what is waiting for me when Jona returns. Overwhelmed and anxious, the weight of what's to come pulls at my body to sleep.

I give in and let the world slip away.

My fingers stretch, reaching for his side of the bed, looking for warmth that isn't there. My hand slides across the cold sheets and sends pangs into my heart. He is gone.

A knock at the door pulls me from my half sleep. Sitting up, I rub the sleep out of my eyes. Another knock. Awake, I realize, *this place is not familiar*, and my heart catches. Plain walls in gray afternoon light. Mattress and clothes that are not mine.

"Juliet?"

Jona. I'm at the Clinic. I exhale in relief, the events of the afternoon coming back to me. With elbows on my knees, I press my palms into my eyes. It's time for the first treatment. I pull my hands away and wipe them on my pants. I fall back onto the pillows and covers. Birds chirp and call from outside the window. Jona knocks again. If I do not get up, he will come in.

You agreed to this, Jules. Get up.

I get up, pulling on a cardigan from the cabinet and slipping on a set of loafers. When I open the door, Jona fills the frame, white coat hanging below his knees, a loose curl in his eyes and tablet in hand.

"Are you ready for your first treatment?" he asks. I nod. "Good." Jona turns to leave, and I follow, the door sliding back into place behind me. Together we walk through the hospitality wing and into the Clinic and all its hallways. He is leading me to the same room as before. Despite my cardigan, I am still cold, my blood just beginning to flow after waking up. I am grateful for the sun-warmed hallways and rays that stream through the glass. The door is open, waiting.

"Get comfortable," he instructs. I do, sliding into the chair, letting my body rest in its curves. Behind us, the door slides shut.

"Nervous?" Jona glances up to me, stealing a look away from his tablet.

"Yes," I admit, the knot in my stomach tightening.

"Most people are for the first one, but after, you'll see there's nothing to be nervous about. Most people really like the feeling of treatment."

My heartbeat is painful again. I can feel it in my whole body. I wonder if Jona can hear it. I wipe my palms on my pants and try to breathe like I had done before. Jona pulls up a recording holo again; its blue grid flashes, then melts away, invisible. With a second swipe, a new holo floats between us, and I am surprised to see myself. It is not the Juliet from my Community profile, but a mirror image of my current self. I am thinner than before, pallid, the skin under my eyes pale and blue. I'm not the person I remember.

"Based on your scans today, here's your treatment plan." Jona swipes his finger, and a new image is shot into the air. A schedule hangs next to my blinking face, labeled with upcoming dates and time increments. "We'll start with ten sessions, treatment twice a week." As Jona continues to explain, layers of the timeline peel apart, each treatment session and chemical make-up of love, side effects, and results noted in depth by the treatment session. As he details each treatment, my image in the holo begins to transform. My face fills out again, color returns to my cheeks, the bags under my eyes disappear, and even the energy carried in my face has changed. *I am Juliet again.*

"… then a final evaluation, confirming full closure of heart wounds and permanent detachment from the source of heartbreak." Jona pulls his eyes from the holo to me. "Is there anything you would like me to go over again?"

"No, I understand."

A few taps on his tablet, and the holo is gone as quick as it appeared. It takes a moment for me to readjust to the room's light.

"Lastly, the cautionaries. Synthetic love is a highly concentrated and powerful neurotic. You may experience side effects during or after treatment, such as disorientation, temporary emotional blunting, restlessness, mood changes, and dependence. On the other end of the spectrum, you may experience temporary euphoria, or feelings of well-being, and absence of pain. If by chance you receive more than your allotted dosage, chances of neurological disorders and similar side effects are possible. We strongly recommend that you adhere strictly to the dosage prescribed, and check in with us if you think you may need an adjustment. Do you acknowledge this, Juliet?"

"Yes."

The room is bathed once more in the checkered grid of the recording holo. It disappears in a blink, logging my response in Jona's tablet.

"Okay," Jona says, pleased. "Time for treatment."

I lean into the backrest and try to break down all I've just heard, like determining notes and beats before a performance, hoping to calm myself. He hands me an antiseptic and tells me to swab my wrist.

Jona's voice cuts through my thoughts. "First, you'll be exposed to the root of heartbreak, a reinforcer, then you'll receive an injection." I nod with understanding, worried my voice will shake if I speak. "It's nothing to worry about," he says, sensing my nervousness. "The actual treatment only takes minutes. Okay?"

"Okay."

Jona touches his tablet, then motions for me to scan. I swipe my wrist across the chair's scanner. Above me, a monitor descends from the ceiling, stopping when it is lined up directly in front of me. My shadow reflection stares back. I really am as thin and sickly as the holo shows.

"The database found him quick," says Jona. He continues moving around me, calibrating the machine and positioning my arm. I don't know what he's doing, or what he says after that. The lights dim, and the monitor comes alive. I barely notice when he slips out of the room, because suddenly, *he* is in front of me.

He still looks as charming as my memory frames him. Handsome and robust, blond-haired and blue-eyed. My cheeks flush at the sight of him, and my heart plummets. *He is no longer mine.* Longing weighs inside me, dense and consuming, as if my chest is lead. Tears brim in my eyes. It takes only one look, and I remember every memory at once. How much I love him and miss him. Then a prick hits my wrist, and a cool sensation floods my veins. My muscles grow heavy, my body turns slack. I fight it for a second, but I am pulled away.

I'm chewing on the ends of my fingernails, spitting keratin onto the wooden floor. It's the only tick that releases some nerves before a performance. Through the heavy curtains, I can see a sliver of the auditorium. Under my touch, the maroon fabric sways like it has been moved by a breeze. It's a full house. Every seat is occupied, and the hushed chatter of the audience echoes off the walls and back to me in a continuous buzz. In the sea of people, the grand contributors stand out, their attire catching the light. They are here to witness the potential newest addition, like celebrating like, dressed in fine clothing granted only to grand contributors, setting them apart from the rest of the Community. But they are all here anticipating the same thing: history. If the council chooses to grant me a doctorate, not only would I be the first grand artist in a decade and a half, but the youngest grand contributor in our history.

Above, a chandelier gleams, catching and fracturing the auditorium's light, magnificent and elegant, one thousand crystals suspended below the hand-painted ceiling. There is a soft touch on my back, telling me it's time.

Every lesson has led to this—every minute with my friends or mom that I have sacrificed. All the other paths I could have taken with my life, all the other people I could have been ... but I chose this. I pull my shoulders back, raise my chin, and resist the urge to wipe my palms on my dress. The lights dim, and the chatter dies. Silence and anticipation hang in the air. I walk out on stage, gaze focused on the piano, and sit at its bench. I run my fingers over the keys, careful not to emit a note into the quiet auditorium. One shaky breath in...

Just play, Jules.

In one controlled exhale, I empty my lungs. The seconds draw themselves out, my pulse thumping under my skin. Like clockwork, a performance ritual, I play the opening lines before I breathe back in, ensuring steady hands. And once I get going, there will be no mistakes. The first notes ring out into the silent space. Clear and loud, it fills the room. It starts small, simple, and unexpectant, to relax the listeners. Then it changes, deeply and subtly. Any thoughts that this will be a simple piece is wiped away. It is meant to evoke the first warm day of spring. Glens and soft greens, a gentle waking up that does not stop. My fingers have to start moving faster. A song is never just notes; it is a story. And I am the artist. *I close my eyes. My fingers hit every note with precision. I am sucked into time as I pour myself into the keys under my fingertips. I don't know how long I play. I play an entire epic. Only when my fingers begin to dance across the exposition, the gentle lull of my melody—the world falling asleep for frost—does my body finally still. I am caught in the beat before the ring of the final key, lost within myself. I press down on the finishing note.*

The world is holding its breath for me, the auditorium frozen in a collective trance. Then I open my eyes—and they erupt into applause. They are on their feet. I can feel my cheeks grow hot. All eyes are on me. The praise is for me. I stand. I spot mom in the audience, and she cannot contain her pride. She is clapping and crying, eyes darting between myself and the council sitting in the first row. She has sacrificed for this too. The beats between my finish and the tallying of their decisions pass quickly in my anticipation. After a quick panel, the head council member comes forward and onto the stage. She says she is proud to announce the youngest grand contributor the community has seen.

The audience grows even louder. I accept their ovation, standing to canvas the auditorium, hands clutched to my chest as I bow. The world falls away when my gaze lands on a boy with strikingly blue eyes I can see even from here. I only see him, sitting there, his eyes glued to me, his strong stance. He gives me a smile, broad and sincere, like he has known me my whole life. My face pulls into a smile in return. Everyone else is background noise. It's like there's a spotlight on him. It's not often you look at someone and know your fates are meant to cross, that they will be deeply intertwined... but ours did.

Off stage, Mom and I are waiting, all smiles as the Community comes to greet me, congratulating me on my new status and ceremonial archive. Greeting the Community after the performance is a rite of passage for grand contributors. I still cannot believe my music has been grand enough to make the archives. The recording of my playing will forever be kept and documented as grand artistry along with the others.

When the boy finds his way to me, my pulse begins to race, heat flushing my cheeks as he winds through the standing crowd. Handsome and confident, he floats between the people, then stops in front of me. He takes the breath from my lungs. He smiles, dazzling and bright, reaching his eyes. He congratulates me, tells me his name, his voice deep and rumbling, "Sky," and that his mother is the reason he's here, a lover of art. "My mother would love to meet you. Please, can I introduce you?" I nod, afraid that words will not form if I try. He motions to the woman behind him, and she steps forward. His mother is as beautiful as him, elegant and perfectly poised with a drink in her hand, the stem of the glass resting gracefully in her grasp. Her dress glitters in the light. I recognize her from the holos: his parents had helped raise the Garden of the Gods. Her eyes light up, and I cannot believe a grand architect is here because of me. Like her son, she offers her congratulations on the accomplishment, then compliments my playing. Her words are honey to me, their attention intoxicating.

"Have you been to the needle yet?" she says, eyes widening with excitement.

"No." I shake my head.

"Perhaps my son can take you! He's a grand contributor as well. It's your night, Juliet. Go celebrate. They are all waiting for you."

Now an archived artist, I'm granted access to the needle, a reward for special contributions like our own to the Community—

art, beauty, transcendence— to our succession. True artists were poets, and poets, like our architects and scientists, were held in high acclaim. I look to Mom, and she nods me on. Wings are beating in my chest. Sky takes my hand in his, warm and soft.

Together, we burst into the night. The air is sweet and clean. My dress catches in the moonlight as if it is made of stars set in a deep navy sky. He grabs my hand, and we run to the needle. It is all so perfect, and I am so happy. One thought thrums through me, echoing and consuming: he will be easy to love.

Coming back is abrupt, like waking suddenly from a dream where you're falling. A labored breath in, and I'm sitting up, chest heaving. *Impossible.* It was a living memory, but just like a dream. I was wrenched back through time, every thought, every detail, just as I remembered it.

"It's done?" I blink at Jona.

"See? Not that bad. First one done." He is checking my heart rate with a hand on my wrist, and his tablet glows with graphs of my vitals. Behind him, the monitor is retracting, all traces of Sky gone. "How are you feeling?"

I don't know how to respond. *I need to see him again.*

Satisfied with my vitals, he pauses to scan my face. My chest is aching now, worse than before, pulsing with pain. We lived a whole romance after that day. I want it back. I want to touch him, talk to him.

Noting my silence, Jona pauses what he is doing, focusing on me. "It's normal to feel disoriented after your first treatment," he says.

I can't catch my breath. Seeing Sky like that had washed it all away. In the small moment of dissociation, I forgot he had left.

The few minutes of Rehab had been like amnesia, wiping the heaviness from my heart and head.

Just for a moment, I had forgotten how much I hurt.

"Just know it's part of the process," Jona continues. "Between treatments, it helps to think about the hurt, to a degree. The sooner you accept treatment, the quicker it will take. It will get better." He waits for a confirmation, so I nod, eyes downcast. "Your next treatment is in two days. We can talk more then, give this a chance to take."

Jona stands, and I do the same. I don't tell him how badly I want to see Sky again.

The lights in the hospitality wing soon shut themselves off, signaling curfew. I'm already growing weary of this room and its walls. Too monotone and isolated. Again, it is giving me too much time to think and reflect on treatment. I feel odd, like something has been cast across my mind, altering my thinking. *The injection has done its job.* The image of synthetic love blocking the receptors during treatment pops into my head; it has re-colored parts of the memory, attempting to strip it of love. During it, I couldn't tell, too immersed in what I was reliving. But now it's like a shadow is trying to pass over the memory. "Emotional blunting," Jona had called it. Funny. The thoughts still come into my head, about Sky and the old disease, but the emotions that follow are not the same. They feel smaller, numb. On the bed, I feel small and more alone than ever.

I press my ear to the sliding door, which hums with the noises from outside. Howls of pain echo from other rooms, raising the hair on my arms. Pain from what? Who knows? A lost child, parent, or friend? Or maybe they are like me, trying to heal an ambient loss. Just like heartache has different faces, so does grief.

I can't listen to it. I return to my bed and swipe across the holo screen until I find a scene that fits how I am feeling, a rolling gray sea. A storm rages in the sky, and waves throw themselves onto the black rocks on shore. It will be enough to drown out the sound of other people's pain.

But not my own.

I head to the bathroom with its large, grouted blue tiles, water and soap nozzles polished to a shine. I strip and enter the shower, letting hot water pound my skin. Seeing Sky in Rehab has brought every feeling, every memory, every moment we were together rushing back. It is a new hell. How can I possibly heal like this? To hang onto the ghost of him … I will be a new Tantalus.

I turn the heat up as hot as it will go, nearly scalding my back. I pretend it will wash all this away. Then, exhausted from the events of the day, I collapse onto the bed. With the mattress sinking under my weight, my body is begging to sleep. It is easy to give in.

I had worried that there would not be enough to do between my first session and the next, but there's no trace of boredom when I wake in the morning. There's a pain in my chest, worse than before, having been reminded of Sky during treatment. I slip back to before, clutching my body to myself in the dark room, weathering the pain. Jona comes in to check on me, tells me a small relapse like this is part of the process, and leaves pills for the pain at my bedside. He tells me that he will check on me again, that our next session will help build a tolerance, and synthetic love will wipe all the hurt away soon.

I don't take the pills. Instead, I let the pain wash over me. *This is why I need treatment. This needs to go away. This is why I'm here.* I steel myself until sleep comes.

"You have to get up." He stares at me. I shut my eyes. I'm so tired. A noise echoes in the room, and I open my eyes. Sophie now lies across from me, curls across her face, eyes wide and full of concern. Her lips part: "Juliet."

Jona's voice startles me awake. My body moves of its own accord. I pull myself up from the bed and to the door. I follow Jona, unable to speak. I am only focused on making it into the treatment room, on getting one foot past the other. I collapse in the chair. This is survival.

Jona checks my heart, tells me something about treatment, but I can't bring myself to listen. The sensation in my chest has stolen all the air from my lungs. My joints are on fire. I am sweating, my body burning, mouth dry and throat sore. When he leaves, I swipe my wrist across the scanner. The monitor descends, and the lights dim. *He* flashes onto the screen, and I think my heart is tearing in two inside me.

When the drug hits my veins, it is stepping into the sea after standing under the scorching sun. My body exhales in relief. The cold spreads to my chest, and quickly my body sheds all its pain. *I am okay.* The cold turns to a pleasant warmth, and I do not fight it this time as I slip away.

Inside the needle, it is quiet. Sky has access too, a grand architect like his parents. I am still in shock at it all, being named a grand contributor, being swept away by Sky, how wonderful and perfect and worth it that it all feels in this moment. As we climb to the highest point in Center, I watch the city lights below turn to pinpricks of light. Every time I feel his eyes on me, I turn to look at him, and he looks away, caught, smiling.

I have never been in love. Sophie says it is unexplainable, that you become one person instead of two. What I am feeling now, it's not love yet. But something deep inside me tells me it will be. I just know.

When the elevator stops and we step out, my heart races at the sight before me. Transparent and circular, the room displays the beaming stars above us and the glowing city below. Clouds float underfoot as if we are suspended in the night air.

All the grand contributors are here, celebrating. I am drunk on wonder and pride; they are all here for me. I have contributed to succession. I have fulfilled my purpose.

The women are in sparkling dresses of every color, bubbling champagne flutes in their hands. The men are dressed in crisp black and white, sharp and elite. Holos of artists perform on loop in several different spaces in the room, positioned masterfully so each song will not overlap with the others, creating different pockets of music in each section at once, pianos and cellos and singers. My holo is at the center of the room.

Sky wastes no time stepping into the room, charming the partygoers, and I do not mind; I am proud to be on his arm. They begin to applaud me again as we step onto the floor, and I blush. I let him steer me through the throng of people. His hand brushes the part of my back that the dress leaves bare. Did he mean to do that? It sends sparks across my skin. I memorize the feeling of his skin just grazing mine, his eyes on me, how he soaks me in and smiles a smile that stretches across his face— a face meant to be captured in stone.

We begin to dance. At first, everyone watches, smiling.

They were this young too once. His hand slips down my bare back, pulling me closer, pressing my body into his own. The perfect curls in my hair spin behind me as I twirl under his arm, only for him to pull me close again.

He leans down as we move, his lips brushing my ear, whispering something to me.

But his words are lost; I can't remember what he said.

Then the room ripples for a fraction of a second, his face a featureless blur, right before it snaps into focus again.

My face stretches into a smile, like that's what it is supposed to do. I reach out and touch his cheek. He holds my hand tighter in his. It is intimate and wonderful. I start to fall. But I can't bring myself to enjoy it like I think I should. My smile wavers, and the room ripples again. There is a small part of me that's grown apprehensive, unbelieving of his smiles and the feelings they stir within me. That part's voice whispers, "Don't believe it," while my girlhood blushes and feels things blooming inside her.

Waking up, I am the stone dropped into a calm surface. It takes a moment to remember where I am, pulled back to the present from the dreamlike state. My heart beats calmly in my chest. My cheeks have warmed, flushed with blood. That same feeling from before has returned, like I am caught between feeling nothing and feeling neutral.

Jona slips back into the room; I meet his eyes easily. I feel full again. "You've gotten past the worst of it. I promise." He moves to conclude his eval. "However, some homework. To keep advancing in treatment, it helps to think about the hurt. Not what you feel in your chest or heart, but emotionally. Accept the healing as it comes, and you'll get more out of each treatment. Sometimes, it can even get patients moved into Therapy sooner."

And out of the Clinic sooner. I decide out of here is what I want. It is the first bright thought in my sea of black.

"I think I can do that," I say aloud.

"I'm glad to hear that." Jona smiles. "You're cleared to go."

As the synthetic love begins to leave my system, I come back down, the emotional blunting wearing off. But I do not sink all the way down to where I was before, in pain and melancholy. I am somewhere in between. For the first time in months, my mind feels sober, like I can think unbiased, without the distraction of love or lies. In my room, I watch the sea in my holo and think.

I've seen progress today in Rehab, in just a second session. But I have reached a crossroads. The contradictions I'm feeling in treatment, each memory it is pulling into my head and rewriting—soon it will rewrite the whole narrative, and my mind will not try to correct it, but accept it. Do I want to accept it? I'd opposed the Clinic this long for a reason, and here I am on the cusp of it working.

I wish I could talk to Sophie, but visitors are not permitted during inpatient stay. I know what she would say anyway: that the science is here for a reason, to just accept the healing. Not understanding why I turned it down in the first place.

But Jona said there is a possibility I can get moved to Therapy sooner, if this is what I want. Would it be wrong to turn back now?

You can do this. Think, Jules.

There is a reason my mind went straight to that day, the day I first met him… If this is where I am meant to start, there is no better place to begin on my own.

I find the archive room Jona noted earlier. Inside, shelves of holos line the walls. Center stands proud outside the bay windows of the rec room. I find the holo directory with ease, scan my wrist across the glass panel, and watch my personal directory pop up. I do not need to scroll long to find the memory. I queue the day Sky and I met, the memory that came to me first in treatment. I close my eyes as the holo bursts with light, its grid scanning the room. I can sense the windows blacking themselves out as the space transforms. When I open my eyes, my heart catches inside me.

The concert hall never loses its grandeur, no matter how many times I soak in its beauty. The lights are dimmed pre-performance, the neat rows of seats untouched, folded up on themselves, waiting for the audience to flood in. The ceiling is composed of murals hand-painted by the most accomplished artists we have, its ornate trim and blazing chandelier from life-times ago, saved from palaces and empires that are now rubble beneath our skyscrapers and complexes. Void of natural light, but built for song, this is a pocket of humanity hidden in our utopia. I wish I could be at the real concert hall now. The grand piano still sits under the spotlight from that day. I glance to the seat where I remember he sat and watched. If I close my eyes, I will be back there on that day.

It helps to think about the hurt.

So, I do.

With a swipe, I fast-forward the holo; bodies move at an unearthly speed. They fill the seats, the lights change, the room freezes when I begin to play. I stop after the council has deemed me the newest grand contributor and the sea of Community members have applauded me off stage—after I have seen Sky in the crowd, and he has risen to come find me.

Reaching out, I touch his cheek, the blue grid of the holo surfaces. The scene pauses at my touch, glowing blue under my fingertips where they hold him, frozen. If only he were truly here … but we have already gone from lovers back to strangers. I look at myself, the girl I was then, happy and brimming with potential. She has no idea what is to come, that his love will turn her inside out. Tears well in my eyes. I just want to feel like I did before, like myself again. If I accept the healing, I will forget his presence in my life. I will be that girl again. But for the science to do its part, so must the heart.

I can't stop looking at her, at me, eyes wide while soaking him in… I remember how excited I was just to be looked at by him. I'm jealous of her. After this encounter, they will live a whole romance. They will grow from strangers into partners, a feat all its own. She still has every touch from him left to experience, every kind word from him, every tomorrow with him. If only I'd known, maybe I could have savored it more. *But I did.* How could I have possibly loved him more? I gave him my heart in my hands.

How can love be there one day and gone the next?

I have no choice. I either lose Sky, or myself.

"I am going to heal," I tell his frozen holo. "I'm going to let you go." I shake my head, consoling myself. "I accept healing," I say. *I have to.* I clutch my chest as he floats away, my heart straining inside me. The holo collapses, leaving the room dark.

REHAB

*   *   *

Treatment quickly becomes a welcome routine, a distraction to throw myself into while I heal. Every session begins with an evaluation where Jona checks the progress of my heart, asks me about side effects, how I'm adjusting, and how treatment is taking. To my surprise, it is. Jona was right: the synthetic love has built up inside me, and my physical pain has dwindled to nothing. In the beginning of Rehab, I saw us over and over, pivotal memories of us in succession. Memories that made me feel deeply for him, priming the way for synthetic love to take root, which it did. I can feel myself changing with treatment. The thoughts surrounding us flow differently in my mind, rewriting and reverting to before I met him.

The memories have started changing too. Instead of seeing the intimate romantic moments, I've started to see the mundane. Like when I would practice in the concert hall, and Sky would sit opposite in the rows of seating, sketching in his notepad. By the end of the memory, I'd forgotten Sky was even there that day; my focus turned to my composing. Or we'd be sitting at a picnic table, Sophie and Elijah across from us, our secondary school friends filling the remaining seats, and the features of Sky's face would begin to blur, like my mind was glitching. He has begun to slip away, melting into background noise. His presence is no longer front and center like Sophie's and Elijah's is. I see our beach days too, our feet dug into the sand, the girls sitting on towels and the boys wrestling in the water. By that treatment, Sky was nothing more than one of the boys splashing in the water. He is turning into a different person, someone I don't know, as if the healing power of time has been condensed and shoved inside me. I begin to focus on the other people in my life, like my friends and my mom. Cautiously, I begin to nurture the seed of hope inside me. Sophie was right: the Clinic, its treatments…

I am healing.

To pass time between sessions, I start rewatching my favorite archives. In my Clinic room, the holo takes up all foot space. This one is of Mom's favorite artist. Handsome and poised, he plays perfectly, musing with his eyes closed, still hitting every key. When I was growing up, she played his archives on repeat. His music had filled the silence of our two-person home and colored my childhood; he is one of my favorites too now. His mind had been deemed grand enough that even his time spent composing has been archived, not just his historic performances. It was a new goal of mine. "My absolute favorite," Mom would say in awe, then turn to me. "Besides you," she would note with motherly pride. He was the reason I learned. Mom would position the holo perfectly on top of our piano in the foyer, then she'd place her hands on top of mine and guide my fingers to follow his until I could do it on my own. Hours, days, weeks, years I put into playing like him, until I could keep up and we were one at the piano. Then I learned the others, greats I'd found while poring through artist archives and holos until there was no option left but to compose. It was my first composition that indoctrinated me as a grand artist.

I hope mom isn't too lonely with my being here. Knowing her, she's probably set my holo on top of the piano in my absence. His holo flickers blue in the room. Frozen mid-crescendo, he has his eyes closed in passion, his head thrown back, hands poised to return to the keys. This is where I like to watch him, not on the stage, but alone, alight with creation. I never tire of his melodies, the way his body muses while he plays or composes. I guess he was someone important to mom—my father, maybe—Rehabbed away, her love for his music some remnant still tucked away inside of her from her severance treatment. Mom said she had me young. I never wanted more growing up, content with our pictures of mother and daughter on our walls. The Community cared for us. *He* was unspoken of, unnamed, only listened to. Who he really is does not matter to me. He is a poet.

A knock at the door pulls me away from him.

"Pause," I tell the holo, unfolding myself from where I had nestled into the sheets to open the door. When I get close enough, it slides open, revealing Jona, stray curls in his eyes and coat pockets bulging as usual.

"Congratulations on reaching the halfway point!" Jona says, extending his hand, a holo in his fingers. "It's a new informational holo. This one outlines the second half of your treatment plan and the transition to Therapy."

I smile like a child, accepting the holo. Chords begin to play in my mind, light and sweet, an alto ballad, like I've caught dancing sun in its notes. Inspired, I'm overwhelmed. I need to play it.

"Is there a piano here?" I ask Jona. I play the notes over in my head, hanging onto them.

"Only holos here." He sighs.

It will have to do.

The desire to create causes something in my chest to flutter.

My hands are swiping, I can't collapse the holo quickly enough, prompting it to project a keyboard. His voice is close to laughter, amusement at my fever to find a piano. "I'll leave you to it, then, and I'll see you at your next treatment."

I nod and look down at the holo in my palms while the door slides shut behind him. I can imagine sliding onto the bench, straightening my back … stretching my fingers over the keys… I hit the first projection key, and it glows under my finger, a blue note shooting into the air, suspended there, its flag an elegant curve on the rippling bars. I can already see the rest of the melody floating behind it. My lips pull into a smile, a thought singing through me: *music has come back to me!*

It doesn't take long for our life together to begin fading from my mind, replaced with the feeling of remorselessness. I watch as the walls of my heart grow sturdy and firm, the strings between thick and rubbery as they pull themselves tight, hugging the surrounding muscle closer. Days turn into weeks. I can get out of bed without struggle, and melodies return to my head, accompanied by the steady tapping of imaginary keys on the side of my leg, composing. The sadness and hurt are melting away like a sandy coast pounded by the waves. The good days begin to creep up on the bad.

At every treatment, my heart begins to beat less at the sight of him filling the monitor. It's a city profile picture, nothing more. I grow used to the feelings synthetic love will leave in me, even looking forward to it. There is no natural chemical process to fill me at the sight of him, no happiness, no excitement, no heartbreak—no love. No more good memories of him. He has melted into the background of my life.

Sky is leaving me.

I decide to find Sophie after her Group Therapy session at noon, knowing she likes to frequent that time slot. The glass is warm on my back while I wait outside the treatment room. I smile at the people passing by. Outside, it is a perfect summer day. The first shadow approaches the door, and it slides open at their presence. Patients begin to pour out, their chatter filling the hall. They exit with rosy cheeks, eyes wide with dilated pupils, making intimate gestures, some hanging on their partners, others smiling goofy, euphoric smiles. As they leave, I catch glimpses of the room. Rows of treatment chairs line its two longest walls, and the monitors are still retracting, tucking themselves neatly away in the ceiling spaces. Drained vials of love wait in the chairs for the technician to come by and pick them up. Inside of them, drops of red run like rain down the sides of the cylinders, emptied of love.

Sophie walks out next to Elijah, their fingers intertwined. Her cheeks are flushed red, her body leaning into his. I don't fight the smile on my face.

"Sophie!"

She turns at my voice, her eyes lighting up. "Jules!" She drops Elijah's hand and engulfs me in a hug. "I kept *begging* Tracy to tell me how you're doing! Seriously! She just keeps telling me, 'I'm sorry, Sophie, but I cannot disclose that information.'" Sophie pours her heart out into my shoulder. How I've missed my friend. Finally needing to come up for air, Sophie pulls away.

"I'm halfway," I tell her softly, proudly. Sophie's eyes widen in glee. Squealing, she grabs my shoulders firmly.

"And you're healing?" she questions me like a mother. I fight the urge to roll my eyes, amused at her manner.

"Yes," I tell her sheepishly.

Another squeal. Elijah steps up next to Sophie.

"You look good, Jules."

"Thank you."

"She's halfway!" Sophie tells Elijah, taking his hand in hers to wrap his arm around her shoulder.

"I'm glad you're doing better," Elijah adds, and I know he means it. Elijah is as much a friend as Sophie. Just as Sophie and I had been inseparable in childhood as companions, she and Elijah now are as partners.

"Me too." I look back at Sophie. "I think we need to celebrate. The garden?"

Sophie pauses. "I'd love nothing more than to go to the garden with you, you know that. But we can't; you're only halfway. But once you're done, we'll spend a whole day there, I promise!" Her smile begins to widen, and her eyes mist over, taken away by the future. "We'll get drinks … and picnic! Elijah can come, the girls from secondary school, our beach friends…"

"Come on, Soph, it's just an afternoon. We'll be out and back before anyone would know. Please?"

Sophie's lips close. She looks over at Elijah, who shrugs back at her.

"Only a few hours. I miss you. I miss *normal*. I *need* sun. Fresh air. I'm doing so well." I grab her hands in mine. "Let's *celebrate*!"

Sophie looks back at Elijah. "I just can't say no to her. I can't."
"You have no problem saying that to me." Elijah laughs.

Sneaking away is easy. Sophie exits the treatment wing first, heading towards the front desk to talk with Tracy. Elijah and I watch the door swing shut, Sophie's fair curls disappearing, and we wait. We wait long enough for Sophie to start a conversation, then step out into the lobby, me at his side. I take a quick look at the desk as we pass. Tracy is soaking up Sophie's words, her smile as wide as ever, Sophie intense and animated like she is. As they are caught up in conversation, Elijah and I stride through the lobby and out into the waiting summer day. Sophie comes out a few minutes later, grinning from ear to ear.

We catch the trans just as it's leaving on its next interval. Sophie kisses Elijah goodbye, promising to see him later, and we step into an open passenger car. My fingers play on the cushioned seat, and I look out the window like a child, waiting for it to pull away, to watch the Clinic disappear behind us. In the trans, the city flashes by. Sun pours through the window, and I relish it, eyes closed, letting it touch my cheek. It's all coming together now. I have shed the old disease like a jacket. I can breathe deeply and without pain. There is peace in my bones.

When the trans pulls up to our stop, I am pulled from my reverie. Sophie and I stand, signaling the door to open. Then we step out onto the pavilion. In front of us, the Garden of the Gods stretches back as far as we can see from where we stand. The gates loom above us, two clean-cut marble columns acting as an archway; beneath it, a walkway into the garden. At our feet, the Community's maxim is impossible to miss, carved into the stone:

WE SUCCEED BECAUSE WE MUST.

"Shall we?" Sophie asks. I nod, sliding my arm into hers, stepping into the garden.

The garden never fails to amaze me. It took every grand architect the community had to create it. In front of us is one long path of stone, like a grid, designed to frame square ponds. Each pond hosts a marble giant as tall as the buildings in Center: the gods. They reach toward the sky, casting vast shadows onto the ground. Perfect rows, perfect carvings, a perfect chronical of our evolution. Intricate and unearthly, the garden stretches back as far as we have documented humanity. The deeper you walk into the garden, the older the statues become. At the very back of the garden sits the oldest recording of humanity, people from ancient civilizations. At the very front stand the people of our time, shoulder to shoulder, smiling in harmony, lines of nanotech striping their wrists. Behind us stand two others with smaller versions of the tablets we use today clutched in their fingers, their stone knuckles bulging around the technology, a desperate grasp, as if it were a tether. We've been told it was—that as a civilization, we were no longer moving forward, no longer *succeeding*, that technology *had* to change, and that we had to evolve with it. That *we succeed because we must.*

I have memories here from growing up, chasing my friends around the stone feet, Sophie's honey-blonde hair whipping in the wind as she ran, our mothers never far. Funny, we are older now. No longer children having passed into the young adulthood ceremony over a year ago, we are entirely new people now. Taller and matured, Sophie even has a band of promise. I am a grand contributor. But looking at my friend, I only see our childhood in her eyes. Looking at me, she must see it too. I smile at that. *We are timeless, just like the gods.*

"Our spot?" Sophie asks, as if she has just snapped out of the garden trance too.

"Our spot," I concur, so we navigate to our favorite plot of grass just beyond the bench where our mothers would sit. Not far off, a child dips her fingers into the pond closest to us, reaching for the pink flower of a lily pad near the edge. The surface ripples with her touch, and the green pad bobs.

We dip our feet in the water, lie on our backs on the grass and bask in the sun, letting UV rays pound our skin. As we lie side by side, our hair fans out like halos, mingling with the grass. We watch the clouds passing above the giants, content next to each other. I had forgotten about warmth like this during my days inside. Isolation in the Clinic has been long, and I am dying for fresh air—any view other than the community room and treatment room.

"So, you're really healing?" Sophie questions, breaking our silence, her freckled arm draped over her eyes to block out the sun.

"Yeah, I am."

"Good. You had me worried. Like, really worried."

A twinge of guilt passes through me.

"You're lucky, you know," I tell her, "you never had to go to Rehab." Sophie has never suffered a broken heart—one of the lucky few.

She gives a small sigh. "I know. I am. We just … decided on forever, you know?" I can hear her smile, thinking of Elijah.

"Mm-hmm. Sky said he didn't want to do that." A frown pulls

at my lips, but I don't let it through. *I am getting past this, past him.* "And I agreed…"

The air between us stills. He has been a sore spot these last few months and weeks, a name not mentioned, a person not thought of. But I think I can finally do it now. "We decided to do it the old way, that we wouldn't need science. The way I thought it was supposed to be." We were two romantics. I don't need to look at Sophie to tell she is wrinkling her nose.

"You also thought you could heal that way." She says it kindly, firmly. I have nothing to say back. Sophie knew my stance, and I knew hers. Sophie is an advocate for our science, the Community. She had no grand feat to contribute, so Sophie decided she would be the best Community member she could be. Earnest and agreeable, Sophie is loved by all. She's made her own mark. Likewise, I am happy with mine, being an artist. Artists are the only real thing left in our perfect, synthetic world. "Just wait till you get to Therapy!" she says. "You get the real stuff then. Your Therapy holo will tell you all about it."

"I wonder what I'll see in Therapy." I won't see Sky; this much I know. "My mom says she just sees me. Her family and friends, the unromantic kinds of love that make you feel important, like familial love. What do you see?"

"If I tell you that, it will spoil your first session. And the first one is *always* the best one!"

"Please? I've had enough surprises. Anyway, we both know you kiss and tell."

She sends a handful of grass at me, and I laugh.

"Well, *clearly* it depends on the person and situation. The 'stimuli' is what they call it. You know, Tracy was telling me the other day that everyone has a slightly different treatment experience. Not one person is the same when it comes to memory and how the mind processes Rehab's detachment or Therapy's reinforcement. It's so cool." Sophie considers for a moment, then a dreamy look passes onto her face. "I see all the good stuff. Like it's on repeat." She blushes, and her face and neck turn red. "Like the first time we realized we were in love with each other … made love … that day at the beach … when we decided on forever. All the best parts."

"Don't you worry we give something up?" I ask. If you just see the same things over and over, feel the same things, become conditioned by it, how would you feel anything else—or know if you are really meant to be?

"What do you mean?" she asks back, her eyes closed to block out the sun. I study her, the flush of pink in her cheek bones, curls wound tight just below her shoulders, not a trace of urgency on her face.

"The Clinic treatments. We *feel* differently with it. Emotions, natural biological processes altered, brain pathways and chemical balances rewired. Losses that should take a lifetime to heal take a month. The absence of lovers, siblings, parents, friends, the sadness of it simply wiped away, forgotten like a dream after waking. And it goes the other way too. If a single choice dictates the rest of your life, what happens when you choose the wrong person as your forever? How would you know if you could be happier, better, with someone else?"

Sophie takes a beat to think. "I don't think so," she finally says. She pushes herself up onto her elbows, looking at the god in front of her. I follow her gaze. "Think of how much we've gained: medicine, technology, affluence … *tranquility*."

I look at the smiling faces of today. Arms around each other, smiles wide—nanotech, holos, and all. Existent. *Here.*

"You're worrying too much about Rehab," Sophie says, and I know my silence eggs her on. "Like I said before, everyone responds to chems differently. They just want the same end goal, I think: the cured heart." Sophie grins at that.

"And you call *me* the romantic," I say, shaking my head playfully and smiling at Soph. She bumps me with her shoulder.

A cloud crosses the sun, obscuring its warmth and turning our green grassy spot gray.

"They know what they're doing… This breakup isn't your battle anymore. The Community did that… Our science did that," she says, studying her foot as she dips it into the pool.

I'm not sure Sophie sees what I do. The garden is not a display of our evolution. We have already given up pieces of ourselves; the garden and its gods are a testament to that, not the fruit of our succession.

We watch ripples in the water turn to stillness.

"We'd better get back," she says.

"Yeah, I agree." As much as it pains me.

Getting to her feet, Sophie extends her hand, and I take it. I brush the grass off my pants and shirt. I take in the garden one more time before leaving. Another four weeks inside the Clinic; that's it. Then I'll be healed and free to roam the city again, free to compose and play again.

Other community members walk the garden paths. Children chase on another, darting between waterways, their parents calling out. My observation stops at a pair of familiar shoulders, his back turned to me while they look on at the god in front of them. *Not again,* I think. I thought I was past this, seeing ghosts on the street. But something keeps me from looking away, the shoulders hold the same broad stature I once knew so well, his back the same proud and sturdy posture. The same bright hair. The same, the same, *the same*. All of me stops in that moment; my chest does not rise with breath, and my heart does not beat.

He turns, the sun bright on his face.

Sky.

The slant of his jaw, the slope of his cheekbones, the face I'd looked into and looked into and found love staring back. I watch him blink, then turn his head towards me. He freezes, as still as the god behind him. His eyes soften with something I cannot place. From where I stand, their blue matches both the pond's depths and the sky behind him. He starts walking towards me, and my heart is beating again, trapped between my ribs. As he approaches Sophie and me, his lips part to speak.

"Hi."

"Hi." My heart pounds. *I can do this*. It's just a conversation. I can handle this.

"Hi, Sophie." He turns to Soph at my side, and she gives him a polite nod back.

"It's been a while," I say.

"Yeah." He says back. "How are you?" He brings his hand to his head, nervous. After all of our time together, I've never seen him nervous before.

"Well," I say. I don't lie.

"Really?" He melts then, like he's relieved.

"Yeah," I say with a soft laugh back. "I'm still composing." I want him to know I really am okay. "What came of your statues?" I ask back.

His eyes light up. "Under review by the council. Right now, actually."

"That's amazing." My words still hold all the hope I had for him then.

"Thank you." His face blushes lightly. We slide back into a rhythm I'd forgotten was ours. A small smile spreads across his face, and I welcome the feeling growing inside me: hope.

I start feeling so well that I smile too—just as a hand slides into his. A short girl sidles up next to him. She is beaming, gushing about something her free hand is gesturing to, but I cannot hear anything over the rushing in my ears. His eyes tear away from mine, his cheeks flushed red. He does not let go of her hand. Something still buried deep inside me, rooted in our relationship that has been dwindling with Rehab, ignites.

He is not supposed to love anyone else.

Pain, fresh and overwhelming, tears through me, wiping away all the healing I have believed in until now. Tears spring to my eyes. I feel my chest wilt in on itself. I crumple from the inside out. Sophie has stopped breathing next to me.

The girl looks between all of us, trying to understand, her smile wavering. He starts to speak, but I shake my head and cut him off, my words as fragile sounding as I feel. "We have to go." Backing away, I turn on my heels and push through the garden, leaving Sophie no choice but to follow.

The trans ride is quiet on the way back. I hold myself together with my arms. The second its doors part, I am on my feet, hurrying back into the Clinic. Sophie is on my heels, her hand on my arm, trying to stop me, but I can't stop. If I stop, I'll explode.

Inside, Tracy is too preoccupied with the patient at the front desk to see me slip back in.

"Juliet!" Sophie calls after me. But I go where she cannot follow.

I stumble into my bathroom, my breaths short and loud. I hit the wall and slide down it. The pain is so great that I cry out, clutching my chest.

I am dying.

My heart is stopping.

What if it's failing again? *No.* It needs to stay healed. I need love, and I can't wait until my next session. I can't ask Jona; they don't know I left. It *hurts.* It needs to go away.

Using the wall, I pull myself to my feet, wipe my face with my sleeve, and start walking. Keeping my head down and one hand pressed to my chest, I push through the hospitality wing and into the treatment wing, my other hand against the wall to steady myself. I find the Group Therapy room from earlier and hope, *let there be a session.* Rounding the corner, I see a small group of patients, all shuffling into the room. The relief of seeing the room open only holds for a few seconds, until another wave of hurt crashes down on me. I follow the flow of people inside, collapsing into the closest open chair. They seat themselves, already relaxed, still talking and smiling with one another. I pray no one will look over and see me. I do my best to lean back and look like I belong as I expose my wrist on the armchair.

A nurse technician enters. Homely with a kind face, she passes antiseptic wipes to each patient. When she comes to me, I force a smile, taking it from her fingers. She passes as quickly as she came. The lights flash, and the chatter dies then. Every one settles themselves, eyes forward, expectant. I follow what they do. The nurse stands at the end of the room, carefully surveying her patients. Arms move, patients swiping their wrists. I keep up with them, swiping my wrist across the scanner. On cue, monitors descend from the ceiling, and the lights dim completely. My heartbeat is ringing through my body. With each breath, my breastbone aches.

Light bursts into the room, washing over every patient's face. With a prick of the wrist, love floods into me. It is like bursting into light. The sudden coolness changes to heat, and my body grows warm and jittery with the familiar feeling of excitement, affection—of *love*.

The feeling sweeps me along the stars, offers me every tomorrow; its arms are home. The heat of girlish affection blooms within me. I am smitten all over again. What pumps through me now is natural, *real*, the sweetness that comes with the process of bodies functioning.

It wakes me up. The last half year has been nothing but one long and foggy dream.

Love pulls me away.

"Can you tell me now?" I laugh.

"We're almost there." Sky's fingers are pressed to my eyes. He refused to tell me where we were going, making me promise to keep my eyes closed, guiding me in and out of the trans, telling me where to walk and when to step, until now. His chest is pressing against my back. In sync, mine rises and falls as his does. I feel the final breath he takes in before he decides to pull his hands from my eyes.

"Okay. Now you can look." He slips his hands into mine,

holding me while I take in where we are. It is a studio, the floor caked in white sand, a single space bigger than any I've ever seen in Center, a room non-architects are not supposed to enter. The circular walls host scaffolding and tools, tarps half covering the stone structure in the middle of the room. Above us, the ceiling stretches to skyscraper heights, a dome, painted by artists so long ago that they could be found in the near back of the garden. I recognize the mural as God giving life to man. It is fitting for what the room holds. It takes my eyes a moment to adjust in the night light pouring in from the windows high above. The stone in the center is shaped as a person.

"They said I could design the next addition," Sky begins to explain. "They" are his parents—the grand architects who headed the Garden of the Gods project. "Listen, Jules, I can't promise they'll accept them, you know. I'll have to argue for the work, show why it demonstrates our succession, but that doesn't reflect on us..."

I can already see it. Sky does not have to explain himself to me. These gods are different from the others; I can tell from the first glance. I step out of his embrace to study them more closely, my voice echoing in their space.

"Sky, I can already tell." I want him to know that I see him, that he is brilliant. "Their stance..." I want to say "intimate," but it's not the right word... "It's like they seem at peace with one another, content, in harmony. Like it encompasses the peace the Community has strived to achieve since its beginning." Their clothing reflects the newest line we've been given; that much goes unspoken. "The lines of nanotech on their wrists are sleek, less pronounced, improved, like our generations," I note. "And the bands of promise on their fingers, exclamations of

commitment, what our science has achieved, the Clinic processes now perfected." I sidle up next to him, grabbing his hand. "And their faces, so familiar…"

"Two grand contributors," he says. "The youngest grand contributors. The highest achievement in the community. What we strive for. They're—"

"Us." I turn to him, breathless. "Sky, they're brilliant!"

A smile stretches across his face then.

"I told you I'd raise a god for you."

I laugh in disbelief, looking back at them in awe. He has. He's always said he would raise a god after me. Where they stand, they put the painted sky to shame.

"But you're wrong," he says.

"What?"

"They're almost *us."*

"What do you mean?" I look back at them, and now that I've seen it, I can't unsee it: he's captured the hollows of our cheeks perfectly. The way his shoulders set themselves back, the way my hair frames my face and falls to my waist. I turn back to him again, about to protest, and see a flash in his open hand, caught by the moonlight. Two golden bands of promise.

"Every tomorrow looks like you, Juliet. And if all your tomorrows look like me … then I promise forever."

I pick the ring up from his hand and turn it over in my fingers. I cannot imagine a life without Sky. And now I'll never have to.

"Together?" he asks softly.

"Together," I promise.

*   *   *

Coming back is bursting through the surface of water. I can't catch my breath; then a sigh of relief comes. *I am loved.* My head shakes no, as if I'm reminding myself. *It's just the chemicals, Jules.* But with love still pounding in my veins, I don't believe the voice. It felt so real, *still* feels so real.

Everyone is getting up, so I must too. My knees buckle, and I have to steady myself against the wall before moving. It was all so romantic, so perfect. I can't stop the smile spreading on my face. *But it's not real,* that voice whispers again. I shake my head to clear it out. It is real now, in this moment, still high on love. The smiling faces, the rosy cheeks, the intimate postures—I get it now. They are all in love! *Love.* That makes me giggle out loud. No wonder Sophie loves Therapy.

I branch off from the patients walking back to the lobby, walking, floating deeper into the Clinic. A hum of music echoes through the empty hallways. But everyone is gone; this was the last treatment of the day. Tracy will no doubt be smiling as she nods them all goodnight before shutting the Clinic doors. Where is it coming from? My body feels light as air. I can still feel warmth flowing through my veins and in my cheeks, and I can hardly focus on which hallways I am turning down. *Me! The humming is me!*

The warmth has not left my chest; it is a blanket over my whole body, a soothing comfort. There is no pain. No, I feel the opposite. Like I'm whole again, like the world is the way it was before, when I still had him, and he had me. I want to dance while walking through the hospitality wing, twirl in front of the other inpatients as I find my room. In bed, I roll onto my side and stare at the other half. I close my eyes. I am still riding love's high.

If I close my eyes … I am home. This is my bed, the same comforter I've had since I was a child. The four walls are decorated with my achievements, photos, books, holos. *It is before.* If I open my eyes, I'm sure I will find Sky next to me. I can see the rise and fall of his chest, his eyelashes fluttering in sleep.

Oh, how I missed you.

I wake up to the room already bright with the beginning light of day. The light hurts. I roll over and pull the blankets over my eyes. In that brief moment after waking, I struggle to place myself. I feel depleted, something below sober, closer to the old disease. Why? I start tracing my emotions, the events that caused them. Sneaking out. The garden. Seeing Sky. Desperation to make the pain go away. Therapy. *Sky.* Is Sky here? My body bolts straight up, whipping around to see the other side of the bed, but all I see are empty, twisted bedsheets. My chest aches for only a moment until reality straightens me out.

"Shit. *Shit.*" Why did I take the love unprescribed? And not just any love: Group Therapy love. The kind people spend years working up to, one of the strongest prescriptions the Clinic offers. I growl into my hands, pressing them into my eyes until they hurt. My heart starts aching, and I wish it wouldn't. I hate myself for it. My thoughts are something deep and black trying to pull me under. I wince. I can't shake what I felt in Therapy. That night has come back to me so vividly. The comfort, the everpresent ache and hurt in my chest subsiding. I want to feel it again so badly that it hurts. Wouldn't anyone?

But I can't. I've come this far. I can't let this set me back. How can I get back to where I was the day before yesterday?

I turn Sophie's words over in my head. *"All the good stuff, like it's on repeat."*

Synthetic love is just that: synthetic. It isn't as sweet as real love. Real love could wipe it away, as long as synthetic love isn't blocking the brain's receptors for it. It's why one goes through Rehab to forget, then Therapy to remember. I'd thrown myself into Therapy, my stimulus still set as Sky, like it is in Rehab. I just have to get back to Rehab, back to where they are conditioning my love for him away, not reinforcing it like I have accidentally just done, like what Sophie and Elijah go to Therapy for.

I just have to hold on for one more day. Tomorrow will be my next treatment day. But the way I feel now, one day will be hell. Has Sky really moved on? How?

Stop it.

I won't let myself go there. A day. It's all I have to wait. Then I will be okay again. Jona will come get me for my scheduled sessions, and I will shed the Group Therapy room from my mind.

I force myself to my feet and prompt the keyboard with the handheld holo. Outside, the sun is setting. I start with the first songs I was taught to play. I play and play, until the world fades away.

I don't realize it is morning until the walls have grayed in my room, and my whole body is sore. I am exhausted, but pleased that I have not slipped back into my thoughts from Therapy. When Jona comes to the door, I exit before he can make the first knock. He does not need to know that I did not sleep.

I slip into the treatment chair, hoping my system has rid itself of love by now.

The informational holo comes back to me, how treatment is heralded as a perfect science, a balance of biology, chemistry, and psychology. *Yes—a perfect process I have tampered with.*

The routine carries on. He leaves, the monitor descends, and the lights dim. I close my eyes this time. The room lights up in front of me. On cue, the prick hits my wrist, releasing synthetic love into my veins. But it is different this time, stale.

Something is wrong.

Grass sways in the sun, and beyond the hill, the waterways of Center sparkle, catching the light. Sky sits on the hill, uprooting grass with his fingers, waiting, his face downcast, his eyes darkened. The breeze ruffles his hair, and a shadow passes over the sun. I am happy when I spot him, excited, until I get close enough to see that he's upset.

My face falls slightly. I sit next to him on the hill, the grass soft beneath me, and wait for him to speak, content to sit in the silence next to him.

My stomach plummets the longer we sit in silence. Some survival instinct is triggered, some feeling I try to push down and deny. Uneasiness grows as his eyes turn glassy.

"What is it?" I ask him, my voice a whisper. Sky struggles to explain it, how he doesn't entirely understand it, that the feelings he's had for me, the things he's said before, he can't feel them anymore. It is simple as that. His words hit me like a wave of grief. I start crying and can't stop.

This can't be it.

I sob silently next to him, my shoulders shaking. He finally looks at me then, small and broken on the hillside. Seeing me like that, someone he has loved turned into someone he has hurt, it kills Sky. Tears finally flow freely down his face. He pulls me into him with one arm, and I curl myself into his side. Is this really the last time he will hold me? Anguished, I pull away.

"How can I fix it?"

He shakes his head. "It can't be fixed."

"We can go to Therapy," I say desperately, ready to turn myself inside out for him, give up all the pieces of me for him. "Please."

"No—"

"Please!" I move onto my knees, clutching his hands in mine, trying to get his eyes to meet mine. "Please. Please. Let's just go, and it will fix this! We can go to Therapy, and the feelings will come back, I promise!"

He can't look at me then. Silent tears drip to his chin. He puts his face in his hands, shaking his head no. No, no, no.

Coming back, a wave of nausea hits me. I close my eyes, focusing on my breaths. Jona reenters, and I look at the wall. *He can't know.* Jona begins speaking, but I hear nothing, I just see his lips moving. The room is starting to spin.

"Am I cleared?" I ask Jona, hoping it came out normal.

He pauses for a moment; I cut him off mid-sentence. His eyes study mine—*Please don't say anything*—then he nods. I get up and go. My vision doubles on the way to my room, crisscrossing in front of me. It's like I'd feared.

Rehab isn't working. It's doing the opposite. My brain can't uptake the replacement synthetic love like the Rehab holo said it would. Chemical love, the *real* love, is still there.

And I am tempting the fates.

The mix of love, synthetic and chemical, peaks once I am alone in my room. I make it to the bathroom, where I retch into the toilet, but my body does not understand that this is not something it can rid itself of so easily. I collapse onto the floor, pulling my knees to my chest. All the while, I can only think of Sky, and fear for myself.

My heart is beating too fast, fluttering within me. I should find Jona and ask him for help, but my mouth turns sour at the thought. My skin is damp with sweat, but I'm cold—so cold that I begin to shake on the floor. I need the medi-kit. On hands and knees, my body moves to the cabinet, and my fingers shake pulling it out. It crashes open on the floor. In my hands, the holo takes three tries to scan my heart before it can get a steady image. There's something wrong with the way its beating, palpitating; my lip quivers watching it. The room starts to spin. And I've grown so cold that I curl into a ball, knees to chest on the bathroom floor, shivering. I wait for it to pass, praying that it will.

When I wake up, the room is silent. The shadows look darker, and the air is colder. My body shivers on the floor. The pain in my chest is resurfacing as the Clinic's treatment wears off, growing stronger with each second. On shaky legs, I rise to my feet and find the biggest cardigan in the cabinet. The sickness has passed enough for me to think clearly. The conversation on the hilltop plays on loop in my mind. Why did I have to see *that* conversation? After everything that has just happened? After all the progress I've made?

At first, I was shocked. I didn't believe it when he got up off the grass and left me. Then, with each passing day, I grew more and more aware. Reminders of him were everywhere I went; they pushed into my heart like pins every time. His shoulders in a stranger walking down the street, his blond hair in every fair head to catch the sun, strangers' laughter confused with his, the songs he always asked me to play.

While Rehab had convinced me I was falling out of love with him, he was home once, a comfort still. But one look, one moment of locked eyes reopened all of us inside of me. The thoughts and feelings I'd been conditioned to think and respond to. Excitement. Warmth. Safety. Tenderness. The girlhood I had given him. Then I'm underwater again. It only took one look, one slip. It is then I realize: love never leaves you, it only changes form. If you're lucky, it changes into anger, then hate. If you're unlucky, it becomes grief. Ache. Pain. Suffering. Forever.

The feeling in my chest is unbearable. There's so much pain, and it has nowhere to go. This is the burden of being human.

"That's why they made the Clinic!" Sophie's words ring clear in my head.

There is no second thought as I walk through the community room and into the labyrinthine treatment wing. I know what will take the pain away, and right now, that is all that matters. *They have given me the Pandora's box after all, haven't they? Knowing it was in my nature to be curious. It's the Clinic that offers to spoon-feed love to the heartbroken.*

The Clinic is a different place at night. In its moonlit

hallways, my body glows silver, moving on its own toward the Therapy room. It's not an eerie scene, but unearthly. Morals and ethics do not burden me now; logic does not beg me to stay put. Whatever has taken over me is innate.

When I get close enough to the door of the Therapy room, it opens on its own. Inside, the chairs sit in their lines, expectant. I slide into its embrace and swipe my wrist across the scanner. Without the light of day, the monitor is the only light in the room. Its black screen descends in front of me, then the room bursts with light.

The needle slips into my skin, and love floods into me, a spread of warmth that starts in my forearms, then rushes through the rest of me. It fills my chest, warm and comforting. It wipes away all fears and worries. All my pain melts away.

The relief is euphoria.

I only stumble a little bit when standing this time. The wall catches my body, and I push myself upright from it. All my pain has vanished. Every good feeling is filling my heart. Well-being. Happiness. Serotonin. Pleasure. Peace. Dopamine. The bliss state of fullness—love's high.

My eyes take a moment to adjust to the light. Outside, the night light blurs against the door. I float to it. It is a clear sky tonight. Center shines like its own constellation set before the stars surrounding it. The stars in the night sky are so bright and clear and close that they look touchable through the glass walls, like I am walking through them. I blink, and the world shifts. Love pushes through my veins in a second wave, and I am spinning in the sky needle. I am dancing so fast that the stars are blurs of white. Hands tighten on my waist. Music begins to play, and I am so happy I want to sing, but in the halls, I hum. My dress swishes at my sides, and in his arms, I lean my head back, eyes closed in bliss, spinning through the night in love.

"Jules," Sky whispers in my head, *"we're here."*

My eyes flick open. I can't go—not yet. I close them again, back to the fantasy that feels so alive.

"You still love me?" I ask.

"Yes!" He laughs like I am a child and he has been telling me this whole time, and I am just now understanding.

"But that girl…"

He wraps his arms around me, his fingertips finding my bare skin, warm on my back. He pulls me into him, and I swear it feels like I'm home.

"What girl? It's just us."

Just us. For the first time in months, I breathe out, and the world I was holding on my back slips away, freeing me from this Atlas curse. He loves me! And gods, do I love him. He gives me a soft push with his arms, and my fingertips land on my bedroom door so fast that it does not have time to open right away.

I hum our song all the way to the bed, where I collapse onto it, content. I fall into a dreamless sleep.

The Community has grown too trusting—another flaw I cannot unsee. It is the reason why I can float in and out of the Therapy room when I am supposed to be undergoing Rehab. I haven't told Jona that Rehab stopped working days ago, after I'd started walking to the Therapy room at night.

Leaving the treatment room now, it feels different, like the love has built up. Intense waves of contentment and peace are washing over me, one after the other.

In my room, I fall into bed and stretch my hands across the sheets. My fingers twitch next to me, aching for the warmth that's already beginning to slip away. Pushing onto my elbows, I move my hand over the sheets, wind my fingers into them. Warm. Warm as if he had just slipped away.

Soon, Therapy's lovers' high is a whole-body craving. All of me yearns for the escape I have found from all the things I feel too deeply. I count the minutes until Therapy starts. It is a Midas touch, turning my world to gold. Nothing else matters.

I clutch at my chest. It tells me: love cannot wait.

Like Sisyphus, I roll my rock up the hill. I walk down the silent hallways, my reflection gliding next to me, into the shuffle of people moving forward. I settle into the chair. I swipe my wrist.

I roll my rock up the hill.

I walk down the silent hallways.

There is honor in survival.

The line cannot move any slower; I worry I won't get in. It's the last Group Therapy of the day, and I need it, *need love*, desperately.

"Hey." My body flinches at the touch on my shoulder, my head whipping to the side. Blonde curls and fair skin. *Sophie.* I freeze like an animal.

"Soph." I force the word out.

"You're in the Therapy line." She laughs nervously.

"I…" Sophie can't know. She'll try to guilt-trip me into

trusting our science again, or worse, she'll tell Jona and take it all away. My fingers linger over my collarbone. *I will not survive the loss of love a second time.* I glance back at my friend, my stomach curdling. "I have to go." I turn my back to her and walk.

At first, she's stunned; I can see her face in the glass.

"Hey!" she calls out, then she starts walking after me. "Are you okay? Jules, what the hell?"

I do not turn around; I only walk faster towards the hospitality wing, where she cannot follow.

I pace the room. Each second, my pain is worsening. My body is on fire. *I need that love.* What if this is how I die? The fear is sobering. Without Therapy, I can't rid myself of the pain. I try to sleep, to wait out Sophie, to wait for the Group Therapy room to clear for the day.

I plummet through a clear blue sky, the rush of wind, cry of seagulls, and colliding ocean waves filling my ears. My back stings as it cuts through the air, blistered from flying too close to the sun. Weightless, my body is helpless as I fall. Struggling is useless; the ocean will consume me. My body is going to hit the water soon. The impact will displace my limbs, destroy my lungs. Tears roll down my cheeks, flying alongside the feathers as I fall. I crash, and the ocean swallows me. The sun dances on top of the water, casting its pattern onto the world below, shifting shadows across skin and sand, strings of light.

The surface is right there. I can reach it. I fight, swim.

"Juliet!" Sophie calls, her figure above the water, dark and distorted. She reaches her hand into the water, a lifeline. I reach,

clawing upwards to grasp her hand, but the harder I try, the quicker I sink. She keeps calling my name. I keep reaching, keep fighting, but my lungs only fill with water. The sea weighs down on my chest.

"Juliet!" Sky calls now, his arm longer, his reach farther than hers. Sky! But he can't reach me either… He calls my name until his voice is hoarse, and I can no longer see the light, only dark. I stop struggling, my last gulp of air bubbles in front of my face. Here the sea holds me, cold but welcoming, floating me gently to the ocean floor.

I can't breathe.

I wake up grasping at my throat. The pain in my chest has returned, double what it was yesterday. It's so strong that I can hardly breathe.

Love.

Love will fix this. It has to. I roll out of the bed sheets and to my feet.

I remember the way I have walked so many times. I pass through the doors, by the people, along the glass and all its reflections. Turns and straightaways… It is waiting for me on the corner. When I am close enough, the door slides open, welcoming me. I slide into the chair. My chest is tight, my heart heavy, laden as if each beat is a chore. With a shaking hand, I slide my wrist across the scanner.

What is love, if not choosing it every day?

There is a world just out of my grasp—a world of soft whites and warm sun. There, he is moving about, hazy and carefree. I start reaching for him, but he is where I cannot go.

REHAB

* * *

Coming back, a wail sticks in my throat. The rush floods me, my body falling back into the headrest. My head floats with love. The world slows down. I take one breath at a time, anchoring my thoughts on the steady inhaling and exhaling of my lungs. *Stay here, Jules. Stay here…* My mind reels and my heartbeat slows as the world tries to pull itself from under my feet. *Stay here…* The chair cradles my body kindly, as if it never wants me to leave—a lover's embrace. I force my eyes open, fighting sleep. My heart is steady now, I think, but tired, *so tired*. One dose won't be enough. I need another. One more will make it go away.

I swipe my wrist a second time, closing my eyes while the lights dim, resting for just a moment. This time I do not feel the needle slide into my wrist. Between my breaths, light bursts in front of me. I force my leaden eyes open to see Sky's blonde hair smoothed back in a wavy fashion, eyes strikingly blue, and —that smile.

The pain in my heart melts away, and I breathe with ease.

His eyes close, then open. Seeing me, he begins to reach, his hand outstretched—for me!

Someone calls my name.

I am growing cold.

My heart begs for rest.

His fingers are cast wide, reaching…

I come to with a gasp, sitting straight up, my heart beating out of my chest. Someone is shaking my arm, bringing my body back to consciousness.

"*Jules?*" *He is framed by the sun behind him.*

"Sky?" He's here! *Relief washes over me when I see him in the treatment room. But the room is different this time, wall-less, and there is a perfect blue sky behind him. He's standing over me like he never left my side. He calms my heart in an instant, wipes away each terrible thought, replacing every worry with ease. Nothing can touch me here. His eyes are pained, yet he smiles, happy. Happy that I have not yet left him, that he got to me at the perfect time before something bad could happ—*

Did it?

"I didn't mean for it to go this far," I say, shaking my head. *"All the things I did... Rejecting the Clinic guidelines, taking advantage of what has been given to me..."* I blink at him, holding a hand to my mouth, tears brimming in my eyes. All the things I did to qualm my pain.

"No, no, no, hey..." Sky grasps my face in both his hands, his fingertips so warm and familiar against my cheeks.

"I tried to reach you..." I clutch his hands, trying to make him understand, searching his eyes, but tears stop me from saying the rest.

"Hey..."

"I didn't mean to—" I begin, overwhelmed, but he stops me to say something more important: *"Hey, it's okay."* He's forgiven me. It's all okay now. *He smiles at me warmly, holding a single hand to my cheek. "You foolish girl." He grins widely at me, only the way those in love can do. "Come on. Let's go," he says, wrapping his hand endearingly around the nape of my neck, pressing cool beads of sweat and hair against it.*

"Go?"

He nods, yes.

"Together?"

"Together," he says warmly, his smile dazzling, taking my hand in his, our fingers finding the spots between one another's like they always have. "Come on." He grasps my hand, our two bands of promise side by side, shining in the light. I want nothing more than to leave with him. It's all I've ever wanted. I will be okay now. At last, my heart can rest. *Finally, I am healthy. Glowing. Healed. Complete. He pulls me from the chair.*

After

Sophie

I think Jona is talking next to me, but I'm not sure; his voice is too far away to identify words.

It's my fault.

The guilt is hollowing me out like running water carves out canyons. It's stolen my sleep. Each thought is penance for what happened. Shadows are dancing against the treatment room door. They twist themselves into the shape of her, and I can't look. Panic is building inside me.

"Sophie," Jona prompts softly, wiping the disinfectant across my wrist, "we're going to start in just a moment. It's a little different than Therapy, okay?"

I'm afraid of the monitor. I don't want it to turn on, but it's already descended on its track and positioned itself in front of me. My gut twists. Sobs are clogging my throat. *I can't. I don't want to see her.* The tears brim, stinging my eyes. I blink, and they fall, splattering my pants in dark blots of gray. The lights start to dim, and Jona is gone.

I can't. I can't I can't I can't...

The screen bursts with light in the dark room, splashing all her colors across me as if she were still here. Gray-eyed like the tales of Athena, sweeping fair hair that made her look divine in any room, the same face I'd spent nineteen years loving. There is a sob stuck inside me, but it has no time to come out—a prick hits my wrist, and the world is pulled away.

Pushing through the Clinic, I become more and more determined with each step. I am going to find Jules and confront her, ask what is going on, and see that she is okay. If she isn't, I will make her get help again. I pass the same corner from two turns ago and curse under my breath. I want to throw my fist through the glass wall. This place is worse than a maze, a true labyrinth. When I finally push into the hospitality wing behind another patient, I stomp past them and through the common room, scanning the space until I see the patient rooms. I check each door, looking for her name. When I find it, I knock, then wait, hoping no passersby will realize I'm out of place.

"Hey, it's me. Can you open the door?"

Silence. Cupping my hands, I press my face to the frosted glass, hoping to make something out inside. A familiar red light pulsates in the room. I can't make it out, but I know what it is.

It's a medi-kit.

My heart begins to pick up, and my palms sweat. "Juliet, if you're in there, please say something," I say with shaky breath. An acrid feeling starts seeping into my stomach. "I'm just checking on you. Say you're okay, and I'll go."

Nothing. The medi-kit beats on steadily.

She's not in there.

Jules, what did you do?

My feet fly as I run through the Clinic, pushing aside friends and confused nurse technicians as they grab at my clothes and arms, begging me to slow down, to stop, to tell them what's wrong, but I can't. Please don't let something bad have happened… *I burst through the hospitality doors and into the Clinic. On either side of me, treatment rooms loom in the wings, their lights off in disuse.*

With burning legs and lungs, I pump my arms harder,

careening around the corner, slamming myself into the wall as I push forward to the next wing.

Lights!

I frantically peer into each door, past their frosted windows, searching, looking for her. There, at the end of the hall, I see it: a single room with more light pushing out from under the door than all others. The Group Therapy room.

Juliet.

My lungs are on fire when I slam into the door. It won't open, but through the obscured glass I can see her, the outline of my friend, lying in the chair, still.

"Somebody help!" My panicked voice echoes through the hallway. With all the breath I have left, I muster one final plea: "Juliet!"

I pound my hands against the door, my palms flattening against the unwavering glass, the sting of it vibrating up my arm. Over and over, I throw my body against the door, knowing.

"Open the door!" I sob, heaving against it with my shoulder, foolishly hoping that at any moment, any show of force will make it give way. She's there, just feet away from me. Why isn't anyone doing anything?

Then Jona careens down the tiled hallway. His mouth is moving, but no sound comes out as he slams into me, pushing me aside, jamming his wrist repeatedly into the scanner, yelling the same word over and over. The impact sends me toppling to the side, and I fall onto my hands and knees. The tiles are cold. It won't open; it's in session. Jona is yelling, throwing himself into it like I was.

I make out his words: "Override, override!" his voice booms.

SOPHIE

The Clinic echoes back to him from inside the room, telling him the treatment session has not yet ended—a sick Prometheus. "Has not yet ended… has not yet ended…" From the floor, I watch him with fading vision, the corners of my sight growing dark. My body is turning cold. My head is light, too light to be safe. My stomach is twisted and full. I think I'm going to be sick.

One more blow, and the door will give way, I know it. Jona's shoulder collides with the door. This time, the metal bends, and the glass cracks like a spiderweb.

Through the sliver of space, I can see everything inside. Her body, stilled in the position in which she had accepted the needle, still in her wrist. Her arm overturned, poised from the injection. Her head is titled back, face waxen, white-blonde hair spilling down her back and shoulders, her pupils wide as if admiring someone who is not there, the faintest smile on her lips in one haunting expression: peace.

I retch between my hands.

I don't know how, but I stand up, willing myself towards the door. Strong hands materialize on me, their fingers encircling my arms, digging into my skin. "Please, I need to get to her!" The hands do not let go. "Please! Let me go!" When they don't, I spew every insult and hurtful word I know. They begin to drag me away. I start kicking, hoping for contact with any of the bodies holding me. Instead, I continue to be pulled away. I need to see Juliet. I think the door completely shatters then, just as Jona pushes into the room and I round the corner, leaving the treatment room and Juliet behind.

* * *

When I come back, all the breath in my lungs is gone. I'm gulping in air like a fish torn from water. Despite the amount of synthetic love they have pumped into me, the feelings are too fresh and too raw to be covered up. The monitor is retracting upwards, the needle pulling out from my wrist. *I can't breathe.* I know what is coming next. I am hurting, *deeply*, but I can't let them take her away. Before the room can close in, I'm up on my feet, pushing through the door. Jona starts to speak in protest. I do not stop.

I am too rattled to leave my room in the hospitality wing. Or move. I can only think. I've always loved our technology, our Community, the things we have achieved. I never questioned or fought it, but championed it. But what happened in that treatment session… It wasn't love they'd pumped into my veins; it was the opposite. After I'd walked away from the room, I'd gone numb to her. Reliving that memory, forced to feel what the Clinic had prompted, my mind and heart split. While the emotions I felt for her fought to fade under chemical love, a voice in my head kept screaming, *No, you love her!* I shiver thinking about it.

After I found Juliet, Elijah had pushed for detachment. Griefstricken, I'd nodded and agreed. But now, I'm not sure I want it anymore. Therapy is one thing, conditioning yourself to love every week… It feels good, right, euphoric, and settling. Rehab is something else entirely. I know what the Clinic will do next; they will make sure chemical love wins, until that part of me no longer believes I cared for her. It's happening too fast.

I want to leave, take a moment to breathe and clear my head from this place. Decide if this is what I want, or if I'm even strong enough to do it. But Elijah has helped signed me in, and our bands of promise mark that we are a partnership. *Joint consent.* The ring on my finger burns as I think about it. I can't sign out on my own, and he would not let me sign out. He wants to see me better, healed first. But he doesn't understand what it is, or what it's doing to me.

I go to the bathroom, where I strip, turn the water knob as far as it will go hot, then sit on the tiled floor, wishing it would wash it all away. I shake with my anger and grief. I cannot hold it all. It comes out as sobs, salt water that streams from my cheeks into my mouth. I scream into the tiled walls. *Wash it away...* I silently beg. ... *Wash it all away...*

The shape of fingers are visibly wrapped around my wrists and arms. They are deep purple and blue, their edges an ugly yellow. Still fresh, they glow in the dimmed bathroom lighting. In the mirror, my body looks too small. I can see my ribs under my skin, becoming more prominent with each passing day, the blue under my eyes darker. The remnants of hurt. I pull my shirt over my head, my arms shaking with the effort.

I look like a ghost.

This is supposed to make me better, I think. I pull the shirt over my chest, hiding the discoloration on my arms.

In the treatment room, I try to fight against the synthetic love, not emotionally prepared to see what is coming, but it's too strong. It's impossible to feel as if I am not there again. As if out of habit, my mind slips back to that memory; it's what they want. Rehab wrenches me back through time, and the treatment room fades from view.

* * *

Elijah and I stride into the Clinic with the other couples. It is such a dreamy notion, that every person here is still in love like we are—that together, we are all choosing love every day. How romantic.

"We could always go to individual rooms today too, if we can't get in," he says. I nod. We could, but like most couples, we generally prefer to do it together. I study the line while we wait to enter.

"Wait, is that—?" I grip his arm, so he turns.

"Is that Jules?"

My friend shuffles forward at the end of the line, following the other patients into the treatment room.

"But she's not out of Rehab yet, right?" I look at Elijah like he has an answer. He shrugs as he looks at her, as confused as I am.

"Grab us spots, okay? I'll be right back."

He squeezes my hand as I go. I already know something is off about her—something unearthly. She doesn't look sick — just the opposite. Like she is too well, touched by something I can't place.

"Hey," I say, touching her shoulder softly. She jumps, spooked. Her face pales when she realizes it's me.

"Soph."

"You're in the Therapy line." I laugh nervously.

"I..." She gapes, her mouth like a fish, trying to find her words. Her eyes dart towards the end of the line disappearing into the treatment room. Her fingers scratch at her wrist for just a second before touching her collarbone. She looks back at me

for the briefest moment, and for a fraction of a second, there is longing in her eyes. As fast as I noticed it, it's gone.

"I have to go." Juliet turns and leaves, walking quickly down the hall.

"Hey!" I call after her, walking fast behind her. "Are you okay?" I know she can hear me, but she doesn't turn around— she just presses forward to the hospitality wing, disappearing where I can't go. "Jules, what the hell?" I call at the closed door.

What is happening to my friend?

My eyes open to the graying light of the treatment room. Triggered, I scan the lingering shadows, searching for her, but there is nothing there. *It was a memory. I am in Rehab. She is gone.* I pull my knees to my chest. *It was a memory. I am in Rehab. She is gone.*

Jona reenters, his mess of curls hanging in his face. I think I'm going to be sick; each time I close my eyes, I see her face.

"I can't keep doing this," I whisper under my breath, hoping Jona will hear. If he does, he does not let it show. My mind goes where Rehab will not, somewhere between the pain of memory and the dissociation of treatment.

It is then, I realize: "I don't want to do this anymore," I say, my heart wrenching in my chest. Jona begins to speak, noting my progress, ignoring my words. I look forward with misty eyes. *Listen to me,* I silently beg. I know what is going to come next. They have exposed me to the hurt; the seed for detachment is next. I eye Jona as his fingers move across the glass screen on his tablet.

"Jona," I start, trying to tell him again. My voice comes out a cracking whisper.

He pauses, then turns to me. We hold each other's gaze for a beat. In it, I can see there is no stopping what I have started. *Are you the only soul left here, alone in this place?*

I get up and leave before Jona can tell me this treatment session has concluded.

Juliet's archive is set on loop in my room. She plays, focused, her hair sweeping over her shoulders and back while her body moves to the music she is creating. Here she is the version of Jules she will forever be. Composed. Quiet. Stunning. I watch her again and again, over and over, memorizing the details of her face, drowning myself further in agony, begging my mind to remember all of her. Every moment spent together, the friendship we spent the entirety of our short lifetimes building. They will clear our holos from the database soon, and then she'll really be gone.

"Come on, you need to accept treatment," says Elijah from outside the door. He hasn't moved since I returned from treatment and refused to leave. That was three days ago.

"No," I say.

The holo turns itself off. In the dark, shadows pace in the corners of the room. I leave my spot on the bed, warm and curved to the indent of my body. On my knees, I reset the holo, and Juliet is before me once more.

"Please, just open the door," says Elijah.

Fine. I wave my hand lazily to trigger the motion sensor, and the door slides open.

"Hey." Elijah gingerly takes my wrists in his hands. They're still sore from where the nurse technicians grabbed me only days ago.

"Don't touch me." I wrench myself from his grasp.

"Come on, Soph." Elijah's patience is wearing thin. Deep inside, there is a small part of me that blooms with satisfaction. *Maybe if you'd listen to me…*

"You're acting like a child," he says.

Bile rises in my mouth. I want to laugh in his face. *A child.*

"But it doesn't matter," I say to him, "because we'll go to Therapy, and it will all go away, *right*?"

"You don't sound like you. You need to get healed. They'll take the pain away."

The room is charged with our words. I start shaking my head, curls shaking bobbing in my face.

Is this what I want? To forget my friend forever if it means the pain will go away?

After a beat, he tilts my head up in his hands. His eyes are wide and remorseful as they scan my face. "You just need to heal. Let the Rehab take." Elijah searches my face, his eyes frantically scanning mine. "Right?" he says more softly, an adult reassuring a child. I nod. "Please, don't fight it."

Don't fight it.

How can I not? It is designed to wipe away the people you love.

I push his hands away. "She's my best friend." I begin to cry. "I can't forget her." *I can't let them take her away. I don't want them to, but I'm afraid I can't stop it now.*

"What if she was right?" I say, fear cutting through my thoughts. "What if, with all this science—what if we *have* gone too far?" It strikes me. *I get it now.* "What have we given up for it?"

"You're not making sense."

Choices, emotions, and connection—the things that make us human. We've traded it all in.

"We've been fighting. Almost every day, for over a year, before all this started," I say, ire in my words. "But it doesn't matter, because we go to *Therapy*. Because we simulate a love that wouldn't otherwise be there."

I watch his face fall, like a wounded dog. For the first time since we started Therapy, my body grows cold at the sight of him.

"But that's why it's there," he insists.

"No. We're meddling in things we shouldn't be," I tell him.

"*What* things?"

"This place. All of this." I flip my palm up to show the silver lines of nanotech on my wrist. In the light of the room, it looks less like technological innovation, and more like scars. "We've flown too close to the sun."

We never should have dared.

I close my eyes. I see Juliet's lifeless body. I see myself, sliding into a Therapy chair after a fight, compelled to forget why Elijah and I do not work. Programmed since birth to believe that this new world is better than what came before. We'd become so enamored with the sun and how it feels to fly that we forgot to fear the fall. What has become of humanity? Too numb, too synthetic to fight suggestion. What is left to separate us from the gods in the garden?

"I don't want to do this anymore," I say with sudden clarity. *Any of it.*

"Don't say that."

"I don't."

He shakes his head as I reach for him; he needs to see me, hear me.

"The Clinic knows what they're doing," says Elijah, throwing my own words back at me and pushing my hands away. "Just let them heal you!" he yells, his anger echoing in the room, and the hairs on my arms rise. He's selfish, afraid he'll lose the version of me he chose for his forever.

"I'll heal without them," I say.

Elijah looks up, shocked. For the first time, it strikes me just how alone Juliet must have felt. I wish I would have known then what I do now. She wouldn't have been alone. She never would have gone there.

"You'll just end up like her. I won't let that happen."

My world is falling apart. I want him gone. Fuck him. I hit him in the chest; I want him out, gone, away. He takes it. I hit him again. When he refuses to move, I start throwing my hands into his chest, each hit packing more force than the last until he finally catches my hands in his.

"Sophie," he says in a voice so soft that it stills me. He pulls me close to him, so that I have no choice but to look into his face. I lock onto his eyes. They are the softest brown. I can't stop my brain from what comes next, to fight the years of Therapy's conditioning. From where I stand, I cannot look away from him while the rest of the world shifts. While he ages, his eyes do not. The space behind him flips like pages in a book. It is us at the beach, us exchanging bands, us, us, us.

Memories and love. I try to remember the fight, all the bad parts of us, that *I don't want this,* but the Clinic's workings overpower me. He's too familiar. He's too much love. But is it the

Clinic? Or is it us? There's no way of knowing anymore.

He's right. I can't do this on my own. It is too late for me. I have no choice but to fold.

"I'm sorry." I sob.

"I know," he murmurs into my hair, holding me close.

Elijah holds my hand while we walk to the treatment room. He's been using the same loophole Juliet did to see me, hanging around post-Therapy. Jona is inside, waiting, sitting with his tablet across his lap. If he disapproves of Elijah, he says nothing. Elijah tells me he'll be waiting outside. I slide into the chair and rest my head. I close my eyes and brush my nanotech across the screen.

Shit.

The two are tense, eyes caught in one another's. Sky walks towards us in the garden, flanked by the gods. I glance at Jules; her pupils are wide, her shoulders stiff.

"Hi," he says.

"Hi," she says back. The two begin to talk, and I stop breathing. Her shoulders drop, and all of her softens. I know that look on her face. He has opened something inside her, whether she can tell yet or not. I can, though.

My stomach turns at that. I curl my hands into fists, my nails biting into my palms. Why did I have to listen to her? Why did she need to leave the Clinic? She's probably just fucked up her Rehab. Seeing him like this, her stimulus is now in a place where synthetic love will not wipe the natural feelings away, conditioning her like it's supposed to. She's supposed to be healing. This isn't healing.

It's my fault. Selfishly, I wanted her back. I wanted her smile to reach her eyes again, her sense of humor to come back, for her to play her piano like she once did. To be my Jules, the one I've known and loved all these years, not this shell loss turned her into. I bite into my cheeks. It's the only thing that keeps me from dragging her away.

Why don't I?

Maybe Juliet will see it clearly now, how she is one of the lucky ones. She is the youngest grand contributor in the history of the Community, and contributing comes easy to her. She has talent. All this potential, and she chooses to stay sad over him?

Meanwhile, I have nothing to give. I have no strength in numbers, or chemistry, or painting, or writing. And it kills me. The best I can do is support, try to turn pessimists like Jules to see the beauty in our society, what the Community offers us. That we have found succession, that our practices aren't something to turn our backs on, but something to embrace.

But even in this, Jules has left me, questioning all of it. I am fighting it all alone without her.

We forget that friends can hurt us too.

For the briefest moment, Juliet's face blurs like ink in water.

I'm breathing hard when I come to, my forehead and back damp with sweat. The monitor moves upwards, the image still there. It disappears in a blink, but not soon enough. The background of her photo blurs into a grey sky, the same shade as her eyes, and I swear I hear our voices, still small and underdeveloped, laughing. I feel breeze on my skin and inhale the hot, sweet scent of summer air. It's all going to leave me now.

And I'm going to let it.

* * *

Elijah and I are sitting in the lobby. I needed out of the hospitality wing, and this is as far as we can get. Sitting next to him, I stare at my arms. The bruises are nearly gone now, phantom lines of light yellow replacing the deep purple marks at the top of my wrist. It's only a matter of time now. My body is piecing itself together; the heart is next in line.

My memory is changing. I know it is Juliet I am forgetting, but I'm gradually becoming more and more at peace with her slipping from my mind. The events of the last few weeks have become one long stretch of black. Something has clicked for detachment during treatment. After last night's sleep, I could hardly recall the events of the past week when I tried—only intrusive thoughts that have worked their way into my consciousness. Vivid images come in sudden flashes: my palms pounding on a treatment room door, the impact vibrating up my arms. The obscured outline of a body behind the door. The sound of glass shattering and my own voice, shrill, piercing, pained, echoing in the hallway. My body shivers at the thought. Elijah puts a hand on my back.

"You okay?" he asks, his face concerned.

"Yeah, just a weird thought… Side effects of Rehab, I think." I'm just not forgetting properly. *Or part of me still doesn't want to forget.* I push the thought away.

"Elijah?" I start, deciding I need to put an end to my frustration, now.

"Yeah?"

"It's going to get better, right?"

Silence hangs in the air between us. I turn and press into him, his arms my most familiar place. He wraps them around my back and sets his chin on my head.

"Yeah, I think it is," he finally says, pulling away so we can look at each other. I try to swallow the lump in my throat. I love Elijah, trust him; all my tomorrows belong to him. He will get me through this. And I love him for that.

"I have to be almost done, right? I have to be close."

"Yeah. You have to be," he echoes, encouraging. "Speaking of, we should probably head over to Rehab, get you into your treatment."

"Yeah." I stand and stretch in the sun. Elijah slips his hand into mine.

Together, we stride into the clinic.

On my fourth week of treatment, I beat Jona to the door. He is surprised when it opens before he can knock.

"I'm ready," I tell him, and I mean it. "I have a good feeling about this one."

It is a perfect summer morning outside. I can hear the birds chirping. By the end of today, I will leave here. I know it; I am close. It makes my heart leap. I will be cleared to go back to Elijah's and my home, out of the hospitality wing and back into the sun. I'll get to see my friends and family again, only coming back for Therapy. I want to race Jona to the treatment room, I am so excited.

I crawl into the chair and sink into its curves. The blue glow of the holo washes over the walls, and I watch it pulsate. With a swipe, Jona zooms in, studying the different tissue and pulsations. It all looks the same to me.

"It looks well." He beams.

My face pulls into a smile. I knew it. "Is today the last one?" I ask.

"Today's the last one." He smiles back, tapping away on his tablet. "Okay. Your final Rehab care settings have been set."

Joy and relief wash over me.

Jona leaves. I swipe my wrist across the screen. The lights begin to dim, and the monitor descends. The prick hits my wrist, and love floods into me.

I let my breath out—and with it, the world slips away.

Everyone I love is here. My parents are admiring the gods in front of them. My sister is playing a game the children play with her partner: she tries to hit his hands before he can move them. My friends sit in a circle, laughing, watching Elijah bounce me on his shoulders while I beg to be let down. He spins me, and I catch a glimpse of her, sitting alone on a nearby hill, close to our spot. She looks content, eyes closed to the sun, the very ends of her hair ruffling in the breeze.

"What are you doing?" I ask, materializing by her side. "Why aren't you down there with everyone?"

Juliet smiles, teeth perfectly straight and balanced, pearly and white. I've always been jealous of her smile. It is the one of the first things you notice about her.

"Because. You already have everyone you need," she says, nudging her chin at all the people I love below. Her fingers tap piano keys only she can see against the side of her leg. A strand of light hair falls in front of her eyes. She pushes it back behind her ear, the way she has done our whole lives. I doubt she even realizes she did it.

"But you're one of them," I think out loud. "Aren't you?"

She smiles knowingly. "I was."

"But I need you."

"You'll be okay. You have Elijah, your family, our friends ... every tomorrow in front of you."

I try and look at her, but my eyes will not focus. I press my palms to them and try to rub it away. She grows bright. She is going to leave. I grab her hand with all my strength. Her presence brightens further—brighter and brighter until it hurts to keep my eyes open.

"Hang on," I beg, pleading. My grasp has slipped to only her fingers. I try to clutch them in mine, but it's like she is falling away. "Please hang on, please." Time is rewinding and playing our life in moments flashing by, every memory in dazzling colors and impossible clarity. I am reliving each one. Playing chase in the Garden of the Gods. Splashing each other at the beach. Sitting in the concert hall, clapping the loudest after she's performed. The engulfing hug she gave me after I showed her my band of promise.

My lifetime in seconds. The rest flies by until it is just her. I focus on her smile.

The girl who I felt lucky to call my friend. The girl who caught everyone in her gravity, who I have loved my whole life.

Her face is replaced with soft white, and all of her slips into the sea of light.

A new feeling overcomes me. Cold is not the right word; it is stale, indifferent. When I open my eyes, I can't remember who I was talking to. Only grass sways next to me, and long stretches of white clouds float by in the sky.

"Every tomorrow in front of you," a voice echoes.

My loved ones call my name. Laughter floats through the air.

I look to where they stand. Their smiles are warm, comforting, familiar, and real, the rush of love a reminder of all those who care for me, who matter to me. In the end, it's all about people. Love is the only important thing that remains. Places, ideals, pasts—that will all fade away.

Not this.

I study my arms like something is supposed to be there, diligently noting each freckle and fair hair. There's only skin, pale and dotted. I rotate my arm in the light, following the blue veins from my wrist to my arm, pulling my shirt sleeve up.

A voice laughs. "What are you doing?"

Elijah. My heart leaps. The familiar rush of serotonin and dopamine floods me.

I slip my hand into his, our fingers finding the spaces between each other's. I soak in his image, curls that always find their way into his eyes, the soft browns of his irises, his caramel skin flushing as his cheeks grin wide. My heart is full, brimming for him.

"Thank you," I say.

"For what?" He holds my hand back. I know every crease and line in that palm. I bring it to my hand and gently kiss it.

"For helping me heal."

Elijah shakes his head, brushing a loose curl from my eye. His fingers are warm against my skin as he tucks it behind my ear.

"Don't thank me for that."

"Forever," I remind him.

"Forever." He says it back like it is breathing for him.

He grabs my hand, and we start walking out of the hospitality wing. I take one final look at Center outside the common room's bay windows.

I look toward the sun, burning orange and pink, rising in the new sky. Stretched before it, the Garden of the Gods stands tall, stone faces smiling in the daylight. Peace fills me, starting in my heart and pushing to the rest of me. Contentment that I am here now, healing and in love with my forever tomorrow. Because of science. The Clinic. The Community. Because of humanity's need to succeed. I finally understand the words engraved in the stone beneath the gods' feet:

We succeed because we must.

"Thank god I'm done. Rehab? Not as fun as Therapy," I note to Elijah. I hold his hand as he leads us out of the treatment wing and towards the lobby. I feel like skipping, a giddy child.

"So, you're all healed now?" he asks playfully.

"Yes." I roll my eyes at him. "The Clinic knows what it's doing." We pass through the double doors. Our reflections follow us in the glass paneling as we walk. I don't know why, but it makes me shiver. I shake off the thought.

"Can we walk?" I ask. "I've been inside so long, I just want to see the city."

"No trans?"

I shake my head no.

"Okay." He kisses my forehead, and warmth blooms in my heart. We push through to the lobby, weaving through the small crowd that just entered. I breathe in deeply, as if I am savoring the Clinic, like I'm leaving and never going to come back. The thought seams silly. *I still have Therapy.*

We pass Tracy and she beams. "All done, Sophie?"

I wrap my hand around Elijah's arm. "All done," I say. We keep walking, the sunlight casting shadows onto the Clinic floor.

We pass patients who are sitting patiently in the waiting room chairs, all with peaceful smiles. *The Clinic did that,* I think pridefully. The main doors open, and warm air rushes in. A boy our age walks past—a glimpse of blonde hair and flash of prominent facial features buried in a sweatshirt hood. Something intangible fills me. At its core, hatred.

"Do I know him?" the question tumbles out. I freeze mid-step, watching the boy pass us, and Elijah collides into me.

"What?"

"That guy. Do I know him?"

"I didn't see him," says Elijah.

I watch the boy move towards the front desk, pulling down his hood once he gets closer. Tracy gives him her signature smile, and I watch her lips move, too far away to hear exactly what they are saying, only scarce words in the lulls between waiting room chatter.

"Come on, let's go," Elijah coaxes, placing his hand on my back, trying to guide me towards the door. I crane my neck around him, trying to catch a glimpse of the boy. *I know him …* but from where? I know I've been conditioned to forget… *But forget what? Who?*

"Come on, Soph." I give in to Elijah's gentle pushing on my arm, urging me forwards, letting him steer me towards the Clinic doors. I can see the bright sun outside, so hot it's casting heat waves off the stone walking paths. I take solace in the thought that I'll forget the boy soon enough and step forwards, signaling the doors to part. As they do, Tracy's words reach me through the lull: "Welcome to the Clinic, Sky."

Rehab is Kenna Kay's first book. For updates, books, and
more, follow @kennakaybooks on Instagram.